Copyright © Stephen Taylor

All rights reserved.

ISBN: 9798396941373

"All rights reserved. No part of this publication may be reproduced, stored in a retrieval system, or transmitted in any form or by any means, electronic, photocopying, mechanical, recording, or otherwise, without the prior permission of the copyright owner.

All characters in this book are fictitious and any resemblance to actual persons living or dead is purely coincidental."

DANNY PEARSON WILL RETURN

For updates about current and upcoming releases, as well as exclusive promotions, visit the authors website at:

www.stephentaylorbooks.com

Also by Stephen Taylor
The Danny Pearson Thriller Series

Snipe
Heavy Traffic
The Timekeepers Box
The Book Signing
Vodka Over London Ice
Execution Of Faith
Who Holds The Power
Alive Until I Die
Sport of Kings
Blood Runs Deep
Command To Kill
No Upper Limit
Leave Nothing To Chance
Won't Stay Dead

Leave Nothing To Chance

Stephen Taylor

ONE

'What do you fancy, champagne?' Danny said, playing with the seat controls in the first class suite on the Emirates plane to Rio de Janeiro.

'Champagne? You?' Nikki said from the suite next to his.

'Only the best for the future Mrs Pearson,' Danny said with a grin.

'Mmm, I like the sound of that,' Nikki said, looking at the engagement ring on her finger.

'You know that doesn't apply to aeroplane travel, right? If your brother's not paying, we're travelling back there in cattle class.'

'That's it. It's over,' Nikki said, pulling a face as she pressed the button to slide the divider up between the two pods.

Danny lowered it back down slowly. He sat up smiling, leaned across and kissed her gently on the lips.

'Ok, you're forgiven,' Nikki said, beaming.

'Are you sure? Because I've still got the receipt, I can

get a refund on that engagement ring.'

Nikki tutted and pushed his head away.

'I'll get the drinks,' Danny said, chuckling as he pressed the call button.

'Yes sir, how can I help you?'

'Can I get a champagne for the lady and a beer for me, please?'

'Certainly, sir, I'll be right back.'

'A beer, and he's back,' Nikki said with a smile.

'You know me. I'm a creature of habit.'

'Yeah, and quite a few of those habits nearly got you killed,' Nikki said quietly, her face turning serious.

'Come on, love, I told you that's all in the past. I'm going to grow old and fat with you. I'll probably lose my hair as well, just so you know.'

Danny looked at her with a deadpan expression, holding her gaze until she cracked and laughed out loud.

'I wonder who Scott's client is. They must be a big player to pay for all this and the five-star hotel for two weeks,' Danny said as the flight attendant returned with the drinks.

'I don't know. Scott just said it was a Brazilian company. He told me, he insisted on first class flight tickets, and the hotel for him and his personal assistant, or he wasn't interested in the job,' Nikki said, sipping the champagne approvingly.

'Jeez, all I got for my hard work and years of service was being shot at and a handshake when I left. I really should have tried harder at school. Anyway, you get that down your neck. I'm off for a pee.'

'Did I ever tell you it's your wit and charm that attracted me to you?' Nikki said, rolling her eyes.

'Really? I thought it was my devilish good looks,' Danny said, giving her a wink as he stood and headed towards the toilets.

As he entered one of the little toilet cubicles located on either side of the aeroplane's galley serving area, he could hear a passenger kicking off at a flight attendant in the business class section of the plane. He ignored it and closed the cubicle door. When he'd finished and stepped out of the door, the argument was still going on.

'What do you mean you won't serve me any more drinks? Look, I paid more for these seats than you earn in a year. You're here to serve me, right? So be a good girl and bloody well serve me. Go on, run along and get me my drink.'

The voice was gruff and arrogant and immediately got Danny's back up, as did the laughter of the party travelling with him.

'Sir, I think you and your party have had quite enough to drink. I would ask you to quiet down and think of the other passengers. I can serve you soft drinks if you wish, but we will not be serving you any more alcohol.'

There were murmurs of discontent as the flight attendant left them, walking past Danny as she entered the galley kitchen. She looked clearly flustered.

'Are you ok?' Danny said.

She took a breath before managing a smile back. 'Yes, I'm ok, occupational hazard. Thank you for asking,' she replied.

Danny smiled back before turning to head back towards his seat. He stopped after only a few feet.

'Oi, I'm not having that. You just embarrassed me in front of my colleagues. Now get us all a drink, on the house, or I'm going to get you fired,' the drunk guy said, following the flight attendant into the galley kitchen and placing his sweaty hand on her shoulder.

'Hey, mate, you shouldn't be in here, it's dangerous,' Danny said, walking up behind him, his arm shooting out as his hand cupped the side of the guy's head. With a quick flex of his muscles, Danny flicked the man's head sideways, cracking the other side into the metal storage boxes that made a wall along one side of the galley kitchen.

'Agh, fuck, you bastard, that bloody hurt. That's assault. You saw that, you're a witness. I'll have him bloody done for that,' the guy shouted, looking at the flight attendant as he rubbed the side of his head vigorously.

'Assault! I didn't see any assault. You're drunk, you lost your balance and banged your head in an area you're not supposed to be in,' Danny said, stepping in to give him a short, hard kidney punch. 'You didn't see any assault, did you, miss?' Danny said, giving the flight attendant a wink.

'No, like this gentleman said, you're drunk and lost your balance,' she said, stepping away from the man as he doubled up.

'Here, let me help you back to your seat,' Danny said,

taking hold of the wheezing man by the arm in a vice-like grip before manoeuvring him back to his seat.

'Bloody hell, you alright, boss?' said one of his party as Danny dumped him down into the seat.

'Who the fuck are you? What did you do to— argh!'

Danny rammed his hand into the guy's crotch and gripped his balls with all his might. The rest of the team jumped back in fright as the guy whimpered, his face turning bright red.

'If I hear another word out of you or any of your mates, I'm going to come back here, rip this armrest off and shove it up where the sun doesn't shine,' Danny growled, staring menacingly at the group. 'Not another word. Do you understand me?'

'Ahh, yes, yes, yes. Please, please, yes,' he nodded painfully.

'Good, enjoy your flight, gentlemen,' Danny said, letting go, his face set like stone and eyes fixed unwaveringly dark and dangerous at them before he turned slowly and walked away.

'Thank you. If there's anything I can get you, just ask,' the flight attendant said as he passed.

'Actually, there is. Have you got any hand sanitiser?' Danny said, looking at his hand with a frown.

'Certainly, sir,' she replied with a smile.

Danny returned to his seat and cracked open the beer.

'Where have you been? I was about to send out a search party,' said Nikki, finishing her champagne.

'Let's just say you might want to use the toilets at the front of the plane,' he said with a grin.

'God, you're disgusting. Why am I marrying you at all?'

'Search me. Have another champagne while I think of an answer.'

TWO

After landing, they made their way through passport control, collected their bags, and headed for the arrivals hall. Scott stood in a cream coloured cotton Armani suit, his floppy sandy coloured hair neatly styled above his Armani sunglasses. He showed a set of perfectly whitened teeth as he smiled at Danny and Nikki coming through customs into the hall.

'Scotty boy, where's the camera? You're doing a shoot for Hello magazine, right?' Danny said with a chuckle.

'Oh, very witty, dear boy, I'm laughing so much my sides are splitting,' Scott said, trying to keep a straight face but failing as it turned into a grin.

'Come here, bruv, give us a hug,' Nikki said, putting her arms around her brother.

'Good to see you, sis. It's nice to know I've got one of you to have an intellectual conversation with,' Scott said, looking puzzled at a group of businessmen glancing nervously at Danny while giving him a wide berth as they exited the terminal building. 'Did you have a pleasant flight?' Scott continued, his eyebrow raised.

'Great thanks. Shall we get going?' Danny said, shaking his head behind Nikki's back to stop Scott from asking what that was all about.

'Yes, I think perhaps we should. This way,' Scott said, steering Nikki away, saying nothing as they walked out of the terminal to a waiting limousine.

'Very nice, Scotty boy,' said Danny, letting Nikki get in ahead of him.

'Courtesy of the Copacabana Palace hotel, a perk for guests staying in the penthouse suites,' Scott said with a smile.

'That's great for you, mate. Does that mean Nikki and I have to get the bus?'

'Not at all. Call me sentimental, Daniel, but I paid the difference and bumped us all up to the penthouse suites. Call it an early wedding present.'

'Ah, thanks bruv,' Nikki said.

'Yeah, thanks Scott. It's appreciated, mate.'

'Well, don't get all soppy on me, it's my pleasure. Plus it's a business trip so it's all tax deductible,' Scott said with a smile.

'So who's the big arse client paying for all this, Scotty boy?' said Danny, looking out the window at the iconic Christ the Redeemer high up on Corcovado mountain.

'Just some giant shipping company, Delgado International something or other. I don't know a lot about them really, other than they want to update the entire company's computer systems, logistics, ordering, accounts, all that sort of thing.'

'What's the schedule?' Nikki said.

'I have a meeting with them in the morning. Meet the clients, discuss their requirements all that sort of thing. Then on Wednesday they're taking me for a tour of the port and shipping facilities. All being well, the contract will be acceptable and I'll be free for the rest of the time.'

'Great, I can't wait to go sightseeing,' Nikki said excitedly.

The limousine followed the long white sands of Copacabana Beach before turning in to stop outside the foyer under the grand white façade of the Copacabana Palace hotel. A man in a smart hotel uniform hurried to the limousine door and opened it for them.

'Welcome to the Copacabana Palace hotel,' he said, while a bellboy headed to the boot to get their bags.

'Thanks, er...?' said Danny.

'José, sir. José de Silva.

'Thank you, José.'

They followed the hotel staff in. Scott waited while Danny and Nikki got their door cards at reception. They moved to the lift and followed the bellboy inside. Danny stood outside, a frown on his face as he looked from the lift to the stairs and back again.

'Come on, it won't bite,' Nikki said, smiling at Danny as he reluctantly got in, trying to look relaxed as it travelled up to the top floor.

'I'm just here in the suite next door. You two get freshened up and I'll see you in the bar in, er, shall we say an hour?' Scott said, opening the door to his room as the hotel porter manoeuvred Nikki and Danny's luggage into their suite.

'Ok, see you in an hour,' Danny said, tipping the porter as he entered the room.

He closed the door as the porter left and stood gobsmacked at the size and splendour of the suite in front of him, with a lounge to one side and a massive bedroom and marble bathroom on the other, all decorated in tasteful whites and greys.

'Wow.'

'Wow bloody wow,' said Nikki, walking out of the lounge onto a large sun terrace overlooking the beach.

Danny followed her out, putting his arms around her as she gazed at the view. 'Well, it beats a Premier Inn. Scott wants to meet us in the bar in an hour, so I'm going to jump into that huge walk-in shower I've just seen in the bathroom.'

'Yeah?' Nikki said as he walked away.

'Oh yeah,' Danny replied, peeling his top off to chuck it on a sun lounger before pushing his trousers down far enough to let his arse cheeks poke out. 'Care to join me?'

'Mmm, well, there's an offer I can't refuse,' she said, heading after him.

An hour and a half later, they entered the bar and headed over to Scott's table.

'Nice of you to make an appearance,' Scott said, giving a little wave to a bartender as they sat down.

'Yeah, sorry, mate, we lost track of time,' Danny said, grinning at Nikki which made her blush.

'Oh god, I'm not going to have two weeks of you two

gazing into each other's eyes like lovesick puppies, am I?'

'I'm happy to gaze into your eyes as well, mate. You know, if you're feeling left out,' Danny said with a chuckle.

'As appealing as that sounds, Daniel, I think I'll pass. Now, what would you like to drink?'

The three of them had a few drinks before eating in the restaurant. Eventually, jet lag from their long journey started to set in, so Danny and Nikki retired to their room.

***

A taxi pulled up in front of the foyer a short time later. Three Hispanic men got out wearing blue suits. Sunglasses covered their dark, coffee bean coloured eyes. Two were twins; young, with a muscular, stocky build, their black hair clipped short. The third man was taller and slimmer, his body language easily singling him out as the man in charge.

'You, be here in the morning, 8 a.m. Wait out front until we come out,' he said, removing his sunglasses to fix his unnerving gaze upon the taxi driver, holding it for a few seconds before finally peeling some notes off a fat roll and passing them to him.

'Sim, Señor Garcia,' the driver said in Portuguese before taking the money.

The taller man calmly slid his sunglasses back on and led the twins up the steps to the entrance. The young doorman, José de Silva, watched them arrive and stood to attention, opening the door for them as they approached.

'Welcome to the Copacabana Palace hotel.'

All three men passed him without acknowledgement and headed for reception. José watched them talk to the hotel manager and collect their room cards. Before leaving, the taller man shook hands with the manager. The exchange of money from the taller man's palm as they shook, and the additional room card the manager slid back over the desk to him didn't go unnoticed by José.

Turning back to look at the taxi pulling away, José recognised the taxi driver. There had been various complaints about him overcharging hotel guests and items of their belongings going missing. Looking back into the foyer, José saw the twins staring back at him, challenging his glance until he looked away. Even though he wasn't looking any more, José knew they were still staring at him as though he were shit on their shoes. José just hoped the taxi driver's latest three passengers had been well overcharged.

THREE

Danny woke up to a warm breeze and a shaft of Brazilian sunshine making its way through the open window and gap in the curtains. He rolled on his back and stared up at the ceiling.

Damn this mattress is comfy.

He turned to face Nikki lying with her bare back towards him, her brown wavy hair lying across her shoulders. He ran his hand gently down her back to rest on her hip.

Life doesn't get much better than this.

'Mmm, morning,' Nikki said, stretching and rolling over to face him.

'Morning,' Danny said, moving in to kiss her.

When they parted, Danny reached over and picked up his old G-Shock watch to see the time.

'We have two options: one, we stay in bed,' Danny said with a cheeky grin. 'Or two, we go and have breakfast with your brother before he heads off for his business meeting.'

'Well, as appealing as option one sounds, we did say we'd see him for breakfast, and as he went to all the trouble of providing us with this wonderful holiday, I think we should.'

'I knew you'd say that. Just time for a quickie then,' Danny said, raising his eyebrows.

'I beg your pardon,' Nikki said in surprise.

'Shower, babe. Why, what did you think I meant?' Danny said, climbing out of bed with a big grin on his face.

'This is what I've got to look forward to,' Nikki said, rolling over to bury her head into the pillow.

'You better believe it, you lucky girl,' Danny shouted back from the bathroom.

Showered and ready, Danny and Nikki stepped out of the suite just in time to see Scott's worried face looking straight at them from inside the lift. He stood sandwiched between the Hispanic-looking twins, while the taller Mr Garcia pressed the ground floor button. Danny instinctively moved in front of Nikki. He noticed one of the twins gripping the top part of Scott's arm. His other hand was hidden behind the base of Scott's spine, probably pushing a gun into his back. All eyes locked on Danny as his face hardened and his intense gaze stared back at them. The lift doors started to close as Danny tensed his body and exploded forward, reaching the lift just as the doors slid shut, leaving Danny thumping his fist into the closed doors in frustration.

'Stay here,' Danny yelled back to a shocked Nikki before shoulder barging the door to the stairs open as he rushed through.

Leaping recklessly down two floors, Danny turned on the landing and looked ahead at a group of old women filling the width of the stairs ahead, blocking his way as they chatted and clicked down every step slowly in their heels. 'Excuse me, ladies.'

No reaction as they talked, oblivious to him.

Oh, come on, I haven't got time for this.

Shifting direction, Danny leaped over the bannister, flying across the void to grab the bannister on the opposite side as the stairs turned back on themselves. A quick flick over the bannister and Danny continued to hurtle down towards the ground floor, ignoring the gasps and shouts of the old women behind him.

***

'Just walk calmly out of the hotel, Mr Miller, and nobody gets hurt,' said Mr Garcia in a low voice, his English perfect with only a hint of an accent.

'What do you want? You're obviously the man in charge. How about you tell this gorilla to unhand me and let's talk this out in a civilised manner,' said Scott, trying to sound braver than he really was.

Garcia didn't answer. The lift doors opened and the twins gripped Scott's arms tighter as they moved him across the foyer and through the entrance doors, a gun pushed deep into his side. Garcia opened the back door of a taxi waiting outside, leaving it for the twins to get in with Scott while he walked around and got into the passenger seat beside the driver.

'The airport, go,' Garcia said to the driver.

Scott looked back towards the foyer just in time to see Danny moving at a hundred miles an hour out from the stairwell, sliding sideways on the shiny marble floor until his feet found grip. He powered forward, legs pumping towards the entrance door still being held open by José the doorman. Shooting through like a bullet from a gun, Danny leaped down the steps just as the taxi driver put the accelerator to the floor. Slapping the side of the taxi as it moved away, Danny reached forward, his fingers millimetres from the door handle before it flew off out of reach. Off balance, Danny tumbled in the road as Garcia and the twins twisted in their seats in surprise.

'Who was that?' Garcia said, his face tense as he looked Scott firmly in the eyes.

'That, dear boy, is your worst nightmare.'

The twins smirked at Scott's remark, but Garcia looked past them out the back window, his eyes fixed on the figure in the road as he got to his feet outside the hotel and stared back at them.

FOUR

'Fuck!' Danny yelled at the top of his voice as he watched the taxi pull away.

A horn sounded behind him as he stood in the middle of the drop-off point outside the hotel. Danny turned slowly. A middle-aged couple in a little Fiat 500 shrank back in their seats at the fury written on his face.

'Out, now!' Danny shouted.

He ran round to the door, pulling the man out of the driving seat while his wife shrieked and leaped out of the passenger side in a panic. Jumping in, Danny crunched the left-hand drive car into gear and floored it. He shot out of the hotel into the road to the sound of shrieking horns, the traffic swerving to avoid him as he screamed the engine in pursuit of the taxi.

Where are you? Fuck, where are you?

'Excuse me, young man, are you the parking valet?'

The voice from the back of the car made Danny jerk the steering and snake down the road. His eyes shot up to the rear-view mirror to see a confused old woman wearing thick glasses that made her eyes look huge as she looked back at him.

'What the—er, yes ma'am, it's a new service, a sightseeing tour of Rio,' Danny said, overtaking the car in front to catch sight of the taxi in the distance.

'Oh, how wonderful, but aren't we travelling rather fast?' she said, gazing out the window.

'It's a whistlestop tour, ma'am, we've got to go fast, there's a lot to see.'

Revving the little car's engine to the max, Danny started to gain on the taxi, eventually tucking in two cars back to follow it. The dual carriageway led them through the Santa Barbara Tunnel before heading into an industrial part of Rio, crossing over a row of railway tracks before the taxi turned and drove up the ramp onto an expressway.

'I say, young man. How much longer will we be? I don't remember Gerald mentioning anything about a tour,' came the old woman's voice from the back, surprising Danny for a second time; while concentrating on the taxi, he'd completely forgotten she was there.

'Gerald?'

'Yes, my son, Gerald Crompton. I'm here with him and his wife.'

'Ah yes, Mr Crompton. He booked the tour in advance. He thought you might like to see the city. It won't be much longer,' Danny said, trying to keep her calm.

***

'Hey, I think we're being followed,' said the taxi driver, his eyes flicking to the rear-view mirror every few seconds to catch a glimpse of the Fiat 500.

It mirrored his every turn and overtake, always remaining a car or two back.

'Where?' Garcia said, twisting in his chair to look past Scott out the back window.

'The grey Fiat, tucked in two cars back.'

'Are you sure?'

'Watch,' said the driver, indicating before pulling out and overtaking the car in front.

Two cars back, Danny did the same, indicating before accelerating to overtake a couple of cars, eventually pulling in to sit one car behind the taxi.

'It's him, the man from the hotel. You, who is he? Eh? What is he, your bodyguard?' Garcia said to Scott, a hint of apprehension in his voice.

'I told you. He's your worst nightmare. Now, if you would be so kind as to stop the vehicle and let me out, I promise that none of you will be hurt and we can put this misunderstanding behind us,' Scott said, looking Garcia in the eye as he spoke, putting on as much false bravado as he could muster.

Garcia looked at one of the twins and gave a small nod. Before Scott could blink, a fist of steel cracked him in the side of his face. Scott tasted blood in his mouth where the lining of his cheek cut on his teeth.

'Who is he?' Garcia said again. This time, the other twin placed the barrel of his gun against Scott's temple.

'My dear fellow, I'm not stupid. As you went to all this trouble to kidnap me, I'm assuming you want me alive for some reason,' Scott said, looking defiantly back at Garcia.

Garcia's face softened a little, then he smiled back. 'Very well,' he said, turning away from Scott to address the driver. 'Pull off at the next exit. It's time to get rid of our, what did you say? Worst nightmare.'

***

The taxi indicated and pulled off the expressway. Danny indicated and followed around fifty metres back, speeding up a little when the off ramp turned sharply, obscuring his view of the taxi up ahead. As the road straightened up, Danny was surprised to see the taxi had accelerated away and was turning into an industrial estate a hundred metres ahead on the right. Worried about losing them, Danny hammered the little car after them, the tyres squealing as he took the right turn at speed.

He knew immediately it was a mistake when he saw the taxi had stopped ahead of him. The twins were standing either side of the car, their guns up ahead of them in locked arms, faces devoid of emotion as their cold dark eyes targeted him along the gun sights. They started firing in a controlled, alternating rhythm.

'Get down!' Danny shouted to Mrs Crompton in the back, sliding himself low in the seat.

'What was that, my dear?'

Bullet after bullet punched through the windscreen, popped holes in the bodywork and obliterated the mirrors. Instinct kicking in, Danny yanked the steering wheel to the side, sliding the tiny car sideways through an open loading bay door to the right. The rear corner of the car smashed into the frame of the door as it entered, sending the car spinning on the polished concrete floor of the warehouse, before it crashed into a pile of wooden pallets as employees screamed and dived for cover.

'You ok, Mrs Crompton?' Danny said, swinging around, hoping she hadn't been hit.

'Oh my, was that part of the tour?' she said, pulling herself back upright, glasses half hanging off her face.

Without answering, Danny kicked the bent driver's door open and leaped out. He grabbed a metal crowbar by the pallets and ran full pelt for the door, ignoring the shouts in Portuguese from the workers. Danny threw his back against the brickwork by the loading door. Hearing a car accelerating away, he poked his head out for a look, only to see the taxi disappearing out of sight in the distance.

'Aargh, fuck!' Danny yelled, hurling the crowbar to the floor in frustration.

After a few moments he composed himself and turned and walked past the workers who were eying him nervously as he got back into the Fiat. Grinding it into reverse, Danny pulled it free of the pallets and reversed it out of the warehouse, steam billowing from under the bonnet with the nearside tyre screeching on the bent wing as he ground it into first and limped back the way they came.

'Can we go back to the hotel now?'

'Yes, Mrs Crompton, tour's over.'

FIVE

Danny arrived back at the hotel and drove around several police cars parked at odd angles in the car park. Rolling to a stop by the foyer, the engine dying before he could turn it off, Danny managed to help a shaky Mrs Crompton out of the car before two officers grabbed him and put him in handcuffs. A million miles an hour conversation between them, Mrs Crompton, her son and her daughter-in-law proceeded to take place in Portuguese and broken English, complete with lots of gesticulating and pointing between him and the wrecked Fiat. A shout stopped them in their tracks as a man in a cream suit came out of the hotel with Nikki beside him.

'Mr Pearson, Detective Lucas Souza. If you wouldn't mind getting into the police car, we're going to take everyone to the station to sort this out.'

'Look, Detective, I haven't got time for this. My friend's been kidnapped and I need to find him before the trail goes cold,' Danny said, irritated by the police interference.

'Of course, Mr Pearson, and we will look into the disappearance of you friend in due course, but first we need to collect all the facts and decide what we are going to do about the abduction of Mrs Crompton and the theft of this vehicle,' Detective Souza said nodding his head for the officers to put Danny in the back of the police car.

'Nikki, call Edward Jenkins. Tell him what's happened, and tell him to call Simon to get me out. Don't worry, I'll be back soon,' Danny shouted across to Nikki.

'Ok, what's happened to Scott?'

'Stay here and call Edward. We'll talk when I get back.'

With that, the police cars and Detective Souza left with Danny and the Cromptons.

***

The interview room was depressingly grey, hot and oppressive. Danny sat arms folded, his face set in a frown as his dark eyes followed Detective Souza coming back into the room.

'Well?'

'The employees at the warehouse and Mrs Crompton corroborated your story. You crashed the car to avoid gunfire from the men who took your friend.'

'I told you that an hour ago. What are you doing to find Scott?' Danny growled back.

The door opened before Detective Souza could answer. An officer entered and whispered in his ear before standing back out of the way.

'Excuse me,' he said, getting up and leaving the room.

Twenty minutes later the door opened and a short, podgy, middle-aged man, sweating profusely in a crumpled suit, entered and sat down opposite Danny.

'Lawrence Milton, British embassy. You're free to go, Mr Pearson,' he said in an overly English accent.

'What about the abduction of Mrs Crompton and car theft charges?' Danny asked, slowly getting out of his seat.

'Ah, good news. The Cromptons have dropped all charges. Once I explained about your friend Mr Miller's abduction and your service to Great Britain, they were most amenable. Plus, I've been instructed to take care of their car with their car rental company, and pay for their hotel bill, courtesy of His Majesty's government.'

'Mmm amenable, I bet they were.'

'Oh, and I have a message from on high. Someone from MI6, a man called Simon? He didn't offer a surname, just told me to say you owe him one. Don't ask me what that means. I'm just the messenger,' Lawrence said with a smile.

'What's happening about Scott?' Danny said, turning serious.

'Ah, I'm afraid that's a little trickier. Unfortunately, the licence plate number you gave them for the taxi turned out to be fake. It belongs to a totally different vehicle. You'll have to leave your friend's disappearance to Detective Souza. He has all the details and I'm sure he will investigate in a thorough and professional manner. I'm afraid the British embassy has no power to influence the police in their investi—'

'Do you have a car here?' Danny said bluntly, cutting Lawrence short.

'Er, yes, why?'

'Good, you can drive me back to the hotel. Courtesy of His Majesty's government,' Danny said, his expression making it clear he was telling, not asking.

SIX

Danny didn't say much on the journey back to the hotel. He sat gazing out the window, deep in thought. His promise to Nikki that his days being in the firing line were over was weighing heavily on his mind. The people who had taken Scott were serious players and the window of time before the trail to Scott went cold was narrowing with every minute. If he didn't get after them right away, his chances of finding Scott would diminish to zero. He thanked Lawrence, taking a contact card off him as he got out at the hotel foyer, just in case.

José de Silva opened the door for him as he approached. He looked like he wanted to say something, but he caught the hotel manager staring at him from behind the reception counter and clammed up. Danny noticed but carried on inside, ignoring the lift to take the stairs three at a time. When he got to the top floor, he paused to look at the door to Scott's suite before sliding the door key into his own, pushing it open as the lock buzzed. Nikki ran up and hugged him the second he came through the door, tears rolling down her face.

'Hey, hey, it's ok, I'm back now,' Danny said, hugging her back.

'What did the police say about Scott?' she said, pulling herself together.

'Come over here and sit down,' Danny said, leading Nikki to the sofa to sit her down.

He looked her straight in the eye. 'The police won't find Scott. They're too slow, the trail will have gone cold long before they get around to investigating it. If we're going to get him back, I'm going to have to break my promise to you and go after him myself. It's the only way.'

She held his gaze, her mind ticking over what his words meant.

'Get my brother back, whatever it takes,' she finally said.

Danny nodded before moving in to kiss her.

'Be careful,' she said as Danny got up.

'Always am. Stay here. I'll call when I find something,' Danny said.

He grabbed his phone off the side and moved out onto the terrace. Before she could blink, Danny climbed over the railings to hang off the front of the building. He leaped across the side of the hotel to grab and hop over the railings onto the terrace of Scott's suite next door. Without stopping, he pulled the umbrella out of its heavy stand and used the end to punch a hole through the patio doors, rattling it around to clear the millions of glass crystals before stepping inside. Scott's untouched wallet, passport and a pile of spending money still sat on the coffee table next to his expensive laptop, confirming Danny's fears that this wasn't a robbery or about money. This was something else.

Who was his client?

Danny went through Scott's briefcase and found a business card for Delgado International Import Export. He put it in his pocket, along with Scott's spending money.

Now for a word with the doorman.

After leaving the suite by the front door, Danny took the stairs three at a time all the way down to reception. He walked straight up to the manager at the desk.

'Yes sir,' the manager said, seeing him approach.

'Hi, I'm Mr Pearson in the penthouse suite next to Mr Miller. I've just heard breaking glass and people moving around in there. I don't know what kind of half-arsed security you have here, but I think it's being robbed,' said Danny in an overly loud voice, watching the pained look on the manager's face as he nervously looked around, trying to look relaxed at other guests looking towards the disturbance.

'I'm sure you must be mistaken, sir. We've never had that kind of problem at the Copacabana Palace hotel. I assure you I will check it out immediately,' he said, speaking fast before leaving the reception desk.

As soon as he'd gone, Danny turned and headed straight towards the doorman.

'José, isn't it?' Danny said as José opened the door for him.

'Yes sir.'

'What do you know about the men I was chasing this morning?'

José looked around to check no one was paying them attention. 'I don't know who the three gentlemen were. They arrived last night. I saw them slide the manager some money for a room card, maybe for your friend's room.'

'Have you ever seen them here before?'

'No sir.'

'Thank you, José. I guess I'll have a word with your manager,' Danny said, slipping some notes out of his pocket to give to José before shaking his hand.

'I don't think he knows them. I could tell when he greeted them, you learn to read people working the door. Carlos is a very greedy man. They offered him a bribe. He took it.'

'Ok, good to know,' Danny said as he started to move away.

'I know who the taxi driver is,' José said, stopping Danny in his tracks.

'His name is Paulo Fontes, he is not a nice man.'

'Do you know where I can find him?' Danny said, sliding some more notes out of his pocket.

'I do, but I do not want your money. I just hope you find your friend.'

'Where can I find him?'

'In Rocinha, but it can be a dangerous place for a tourist to be wandering about by themselves. If you wait, I finish in twenty minutes, I will take you.'

'Thank you, José, you're a good man,' Danny said, tucking the notes into José's top pocket before he could object.

Looking back, Danny turned his attention to the manager heading back to the reception desk.

'Carlos isn't it?'

'Yes sir, Carlos Ferreira, hotel manager,'

Danny took Scott's wedge of spending money out of his pocket and just held it casually in his hand.

'The three gentlemen that arrived last night and left with my friend this morning,' Danny said politely.

'Sir, I've already told the police all I know.'

'Which was nothing, right?'

'Correct, sir,'

'Are you sure there wasn't anything else?' Danny said, peeling off a few notes as he watched Carlos's greedy eyes following the money.

'Well, there was one thing.'

'Go on,' Danny said, sliding the notes across the desk.

Carlos looked around to make sure no one was looking before slipping the notes into his pocket.

'The tall man spoke to me in English. When he left the desk, they didn't speak to each other in Portuguese. They spoke in Spanish with one of the men, the twin, saying I hope they have good coffee in the room. He called it tinto. Tinto is the Colombian word for coffee.'

'Colombian. Ok thank you, Carlos,' Danny said, walking away towards the exit, giving a wink to José as he opened the door for him to leave. Crossing the road, Danny sat on a bench overlooking the beach and waited for José to finish his shift.

SEVEN

The wait for José felt like forever. Danny contemplated popping up to the room to see Nikki, but thought better of it. Time was not on his side. He needed to concentrate and focus. Why would anyone kidnap Scott? If it was for money, they would have been better off kidnapping Nikki and asking for a ransom. People desperate for money wouldn't leave cash and valuables in the hotel room, and what did Colombia have to do with it? Apart from giving himself a headache, he had no answers and was relieved when José finally emerged from the staff exit on the side of the hotel. He nodded over to Danny, who got up and followed him over to his rusty old Nissan. It had once been red but time and the tropical sun had faded it to a dull matt pink.

They drove for just over twenty minutes, heading through a long tunnel passing under one of the high rocky mountains, before coming out the other side and turning back into the district of Rocinha. The district sat nestled between the mountains, a mixture of shanty town and urbanised slum. The three- and four-storey concrete and brick buildings painted in a multitude of bright colours, climbed their way up the steep sides of the mountains that contained them.

'Whereabouts is this Paulo Fontes?' Danny said.

'A garage and taxi depot up there, near where I live,' José said, pointing higher up the steep slopes.

They turned off the main road, its shops and tourist bars nestled under a spaghetti mess of power and telephone cables sprawling along and across the road from overhead. José headed up the ever narrowing streets as he left the tourist area behind and headed into residential housing and small local businesses. Pulling up a little way back from a garage, José pointed out three taxis parked outside, all signed up like the one Danny had chased earlier.

'That's him, Paulo Fontes, in the red T-shirt,' José said, pointing to a life-hardened man in his thirties sitting in a weather-stained old plastic chair by the side of the road in front of the garage. Two other taxi drivers sat beside him next to an equally tatty plastic table, with a ripped pub umbrella poking out the top to keep the hot sunshine off their heads.

'Thanks José, you can go. You've done enough to help,' Danny said, smiling and offering José his hand.

'Ok, but I'll wait here a while, just in case you need me.'

Danny nodded, shook his hand, and got out. He walked on the far side of the vehicles, keeping out of sight until he was opposite the seated men. Paulo looked up to see him, at first in surprise, hopeful of another rich white tourist to rip off, then in recognition of the man chasing him earlier that morning. He stumbled to his feet and started backing away into the garage, shouting something in Portuguese as he went. The other two drivers looking from Danny to Paulo in confusion.

'Where's Scott Miller?' Danny growled, his face like granite, his eyes determined, dark, and dangerous.

'You should get out of here, English, while you still can,' Paulo said as a bunch of mechanics appeared from behind cars, a variety of tools in their hands and looks that said they weren't averse to trouble.

'Last chance, where did you take Scott Miller?' Danny said, watching Paulo edging to the back of the garage while taking in the mechanics in his peripheral vision.

Paulo didn't take the easy option. His eyes flicked to the left as a mechanic came in at Danny, swinging a tyre iron towards his head. The mechanic's movements were slow and clumsy. Danny ducked the swing to give two lightning punches to the body followed by an uppercut, catching the guy under the chin. His head whipped back, followed by his body before he landed flat on his back, the tyre iron clanging around on the oily concrete floor.

Danny's eyes were on an approach from the other side before the man hit the deck. He spun to one side to avoid another mechanic trying to stab him in the neck with a long screwdriver. Grabbing the guy's overalls before he could straighten up for another go, Danny pulled himself in with all his might, tilting his head forward to headbutt the guy on the bridge of his nose. Bone and cartilage disintegrated as the guy's eyes rolled back in his head and he crumpled to the floor. With a trickle of the man's blood running down his forehead, Danny turned slowly to face the last mechanic. He took one look into Danny's face, dropped his hammer and backed out of the garage into the street with his palms up in front of him.

'What the fuck is going on out here?' came a shout from beyond a door at the rear of the garage. A second later, a man with an AK47 rifle in his hands entered the garage workshop.

Ducking down behind a car with its bonnet up, Danny picked up the dropped tyre iron before springing back up and launching it at the man with the rifle. It spun fast through the air, the heavy socket end striking the man squarely between his eyes, sending him to the floor out cold, leaving Paulo in Danny's line of sight as he bolted out the open door.

Ah shit! Why is nothing ever easy?

Taking off after him, with his trainers fighting for grip on the oily concrete, Danny leaped through the open door into a breeze-block corridor behind the workshop. Gaining speed, Danny charged through a still-swinging door at the other end of the corridor, bursting into a room with an armed guard and four women cutting and weighing blocks of cocaine into little plastic bags for dealing. The armed guard was just getting to his feet, alarmed at seeing Paulo run in, then run out of the back door onto the roof terrace. Danny grabbed the end of the table and threw it up in front of the guard with such force it somersaulted, engulfing the room in a thick white cloud of cocaine powder. Leaving the chaos, Danny continued to chase after Paulo out the back door, cocaine powder trailing off his unruly mop of hair like it was on fire. He spotted Paulo just before he disappeared off the edge of the roof, dropping out of sight onto the roof of the house built below them. When Danny reached the edge, Paulo was already leaping onto the next building.

A sea of concrete and tin roofs layered their way down the steep mountainside all the way to the wealthy tower block by the sea in the distance. Jumping down, Danny set off after Paulo, his legs pumping and footsteps booming as he crossed from the concrete onto a tin roof. A few steps forward and a sudden surge of adrenaline hit him. His heart pounded and his mind felt like it was working at double speed. Everything around him looked as though it was moving slower than normal. It took a second before he realised he'd breathed in a hefty amount of cocaine powder when he threw the table over in the cutting room.

Paulo was on the edge of the building below, squatting to jump down onto a lower shop roof that gave him access to a narrow little back street below. On a cocaine high, Danny dived recklessly at Paulo, sending them both off the roof, falling down through the shop's awning to crash onto crates of fruit and veg lining the pavement. Landing on top of Paulo, Danny's body weight transferred through his knee, snapping Paulo's leg halfway between his ankle and knee. Rolling off Paulo as he screamed in pain, Danny grabbed him by the collar. Ignoring the shop owner and bystanders in the street as they scurried away, scared by their violent entrance, Danny dragged Paulo out into the street.

'Where did you take Scott Miller?' Danny yelled, inches from his face, his eyes dilated and a crazed look on his face.

'I can't tell you, they will kill me if I tell you,' Paulo said, pain and fear written on his face.

'I'll fucking kill you if you don't,' Danny growled, grabbing hold of Paulo's ankle and twisting the broken bones around.

Paulo screamed and arched his back as the intense pain crippled him.

'Where did you take him?'

Danny let go of the ankle and let Paulo get a breath.

'Fuck you.'

He grabbed his ankle again, giving it a little tweak.

'No, no, ok. I took them to Jacarepaguá Airport, they got on a private jet.'

'Private jet, going where?' Danny said, twisting the leg a bit.

'Argh, no, they're going to La Vanguardia Airport. It's a couple of hours outside of Bogotá.'

'Who are they and what do they want with him?'

'They work for El Diablo. We all work for him. He supplies the drugs from Colombia. I don't know what they want with him.'

'El Diablo, what? The devil? What's this El Diablo's

real name? Tell me,' Danny said, threatening to twist the ankle again.

'El Diablo, his name is Balthasar.'

A shot rang out before Paulo could say the surname, the bullet entering his temple on one side before ripping a large hole out of the other. Blood and brain sprayed out across the street. Danny turned his head to see the guy from the room full of cocaine standing in the street, pointing a handgun at his head. There was no chance to move out of the way. Danny accepted his fate and stared defiantly as he waited for the trigger to be pulled. Instead, he saw a flash of rusty pink as José drove into the gunman from behind, the impact whipping the man back onto the bonnet. The back of his head hit the windscreen hard, sending cracks starring out from the impact before leaving a blood smear as he continued up and over the top of the car to crumple like a rag doll in the street behind the car.

'Quick, get in,' José said, throwing the passenger door open.

Danny dived into the car, slamming the door shut as José screamed off up the street.

EIGHT

Scott came round to the throbbing hum of jet engines. It took him a while to shake the fuzz out of his head and gain focus on his surroundings. He remembered one twin grabbing his arm in the taxi while the other injected him with something. Then it had been lights out. Sitting in the plush leather seat of a private jet, Scott blinked a few times and looked over at the seats in front of him. The twins sat near the front of the plane. They looked back at him without expression, then turned away, suitably unimpressed.

'Mr Miller, can I get you anything, a drink, some food?' said a voice to his left. The English was perfect, with only a hint of an accent.

Scott looked at the seats opposite. Diego Garcia looked back at him and smiled.

'My dear fellow, I would very much like you to explain exactly what your intentions are,' Scott said, trying to look as brave and confident as he could.

'All in good time, Mr Miller. Try to relax. We are not

here to hurt you. Here, have a drink, it will clear your head. All will be explained when we get to our destination,' Diego said, passing him a bottle of water.

With his mouth feeling like the bottom of a budgie cage, Scott begrudgingly took the bottle and drank some.

'Our destination? Where are you taking me?'

'Colombia, Mr Miller. There's someone there who's really looking forward to meeting you.'

'Colombia! Why the hell are we going to Colombia?'

'All in good time, Mr Miller, all in good time.'

With nowhere to go and nothing he could do while they were in the air, Scott finished the bottle of water and sat back, hoping the faith he had in his best friend wouldn't fail him this time.

How the hell is Daniel going to find me in Colombia?

NINE

'Thank you, José, you didn't have to do that, my friend. I didn't want you put in danger,' Danny said, his head clearing as the cocaine's effects wore off.

'I did not do it for you. Those people infect this place like a disease with their drugs and prostitution rackets. I hate them.'

'Well, thanks anyway. Here, this is for the damage to the car. Can you take me to the Tom Jobim airport?' Danny said, taking a bunch of notes from his jeans and tucking them into José's shirt pocket while he drove so he couldn't refuse it.

'Thank you, but I can't take you looking like that.'

Danny flicked the sun visor down and looked at his reflection. He had white powder in his hair and more stuck to the blood on his forehead, not to mention the blood and fruit stains on his shirt from Paulo and the grocery shop.

'You're right, an airport sniffer dog would have a field day with this lot. Can you take me back to the hotel?'

Danny said, giving José a big grin.

'Ok, no problem.'

Danny pulled his phone out of his pocket and called Nikki.

'Danny, what's happening?' came Nikki's worried response less than half a ring later and before he could get a word in.

'I'm on my way back. Get on your laptop and book us flights to Bogotá, Colombia. Any airline, any seat, the earliest ones available, then start packing. I'll be back in twenty minutes,' Danny said, hanging up before Nikki could answer.

Scrolling through his contacts, he called his friend and Chief of the Secret Intelligence Service, Edward Jenkins.

'Daniel, our man from the embassy got you out of the police station, then.'

'Yeah, thanks, Ed, but that's old news. I need a favour.'

'I'm listening,' Edward replied.

'They've taken Scott out of the country on a private jet to La Vanguardia Airport. It's somewhere outside of Bogotá, Colombia. The men that took him all work for someone nicknamed El Diablo, real name's Balthasar something. He's supplying a shit load of cocaine down here in Rio. I was hoping some of your friends across the pond in the DEA could help us.'

'Leave it with me. I'm assuming you're heading in that direction?'

'Yeah, I'll be on the next flight out of here,' Danny said, looking at this watch.

'Ok, call me when you land,' Edward said, hanging up before Danny could thank him.

'Drop us here, José. I don't want to cause you any more trouble,' said Danny, thinking about what it would look like getting out of José's car outside his place of work.

'Ok, I hope you get your friend back,' José said as Danny got out.

Danny gave him a solemn nod before heading across the road to the hotel. He walked through reception and headed up the stairs, ignoring people's stares at the cocaine, blood and squashed fruit covering his head and torso.

'Oh my god, are you alright?' Nikki said, putting her hands to her face at the sight of blood on Danny's shirt.

'What? Er, yeah, I'm fine, it's not mine. Did you get the flights booked?' Danny said, leaving a trail of dirty clothes across the suite as he stripped off and headed for the shower.

'It wasn't easy, but I managed to get two tickets booked for 5:45 p.m. What's all that white stuff in your hair?' she said, feeling dizzy at the speed everything was happening.

'Cocaine, take a good sniff. You can fly to Bogotá without any tickets,' Danny said, disappearing into the bathroom.

'Whoa, hang on, what, cocaine? Can you just slow it all down and tell me what the hell's going on?' Nikki said, following him.

'Ok, Scott's got himself kidnapped by a bunch of

Colombian heavies. They work for some drug lord called Balthasar something or other. He's nicknamed El Diablo. They drove Scott to the airport and put him on a private jet to Bogotá, Colombia. So that's why we're getting a flight to Bogotá, to get him back,' Danny said, giving her a grin and a wink as he dropped his pants and stepped into the shower.

'Oh, is that all? Well, I don't know why I was worried,' Nikki said, walking out of the bathroom to finish packing.

A few hours later, Danny and Nikki boarded a Latam Airlines flight for Bogotá and settled in for the six-and-a-half-hour journey.

'I hope Scott's ok,' Nikki said, holding Danny's hand tightly as the plane took off.

'Look, they want Scott for a reason, and whatever that reason is, they want him alive and healthy enough to do it,' Danny said, reassuring her.

'What could they possibly want with Scott?'

'Well, he's a computer wizard. Perhaps El Diablo needs help with his tax return,' Danny said in a poor attempt to lighten the mood.

'That's really not helping,' Nikki said with a worried frown.

'Yeah, sorry. Try not to worry, I'll find him and I will get him back.'

'I do worry, I worry that one day your luck's going to run out and I'm going to lose you,' Nikki said, tears filling her eyes.

'Hey, come on, I told you, I'm done with all that. This

is the last time. Get Scott back and that's it. No heroics, ok, I'll be super careful.'

TEN

Scott felt the plane dip as it started its slow descent to La Vanguardia Airport. It circled to line up its approach, Scott looked out the window at the private airfield with its small terminal building and line of hangars and parked light aircraft.

What would Daniel do? If I could knock one of these meatheads out, I could make a break for the terminal building. There's got to be some kind of police or security presence in there.

He looked over at the stocky twins while running through what he'd learned from his half dozen jujitsu classes.

A front snap punch, a small left jab as I prepare for the main strike from the right, then run like the tax man's after me to the terminal building.

The plane touched down on the tarmac as Scott ran through the plan in his head, his confidence growing as it played out perfectly, ending in the authorities arresting Garcia and the twins before hailing him a hero. It taxied past the terminal building, pulling to a halt outside a hangar next to a bulkier nine-seater twin turboprop Piaggio P-180 light aircraft, its pilot nodding to the private jet's pilot from the bottom of his boarding steps as the engines started to wind down. The jet's pilot came out of the cabin and pulled the lever on the aircraft door, lowering it down to form steps to the ground. He stepped away and quickly returned to the cockpit. His paid-for discretion meant he didn't know what was going on, and didn't want to know. Behind him, the twins stepped out onto the tarmac and stood eyeing their surroundings for any sign of trouble.

'After you, Mr Miller,' said Garcia, getting up out of his seat to stand behind Scott.

Ok, old man, this is your chance. It's now or never.

He got up and moved off the plane, pleased to see one of the twins had moved over to the light aircraft while his brother stood facing Scott at the bottom of the steps.

'Ha!' Scott shrieked, twisting his body as he jabbed his left fist into the twin's face before snapping it back. 'Wah!' he yelled, punching again with the right. It was only on the return of his second punch that he registered how much his fists hurt, and how little the man had moved. Scott looked up at the twin's face as he stared angrily back down at him. Taking a leaf out of Danny's book, Scott kicked him in the balls as hard as he could. Leaving the twin doubled-up in pain behind him, Scott took off, running for the terminal building as fast as his legs would take him. He risked a look behind him just before reaching the entrance doors, surprised to see that neither Garcia nor the other twin were giving chase.

They're probably preparing to make a hasty escape and fly out of here in the other aeroplane.

'Help, does anyone speak English? I've been kidnapped, er, secuestrada, I've been secuestrada-ed,' Scott yelled, trying to remember his teach-yourself-Spanish CDs. Spotting two armed security guards and a suited man looking at him strangely from the far side of the room, Scott ran over to them.

'Si Señor, I speak English,' said the suited man with a reassuring smile.

'Thank god. The men out there on the plane, the one that just landed, they kidnapped me in Brazil and flew me here. Quick, arrest them. They're out there now, right now.'

The man said something in Spanish to the guards, who immediately took their guns out of their holsters.

'Show me, Señor …?'

'Miller, Scott Miller.'

'Señor Miller.'

Full of newfound confidence, Scott led the men out of the building and headed towards Garcia and the twins still standing by the light aeroplane.

'That's them, arrest them,' Scott said as they got close.

'You did this to Rico?' the suited man said, looking at the twin with a red patch on his face and a stoop as he cupped his bruised balls.

'Yes, but how did you know his name was Rico?' Scott said, turning to look at the suited man, a sinking feeling in his stomach.

At that point the man laughed loudly while the guards

either side of him grinned. Confused, Scott turned to see Garcia smiling as well.

'Excuse me for having a little fun at your expense. Allow me to introduce myself. Balthasar Delgado, and please, think of yourself as my guest, Mr Miller. Shall we?' Balthasar said, gesturing his hand towards the light aircraft.

'Do I have a choice?' Scott said, looking him in the eye.

'Absolutely not, my friend, but there is an easy way and a hard way we can do this,' Balthasar replied, his mild-mannered façade dropping for a second to reveal a cold, ruthless stare.

Without any other choice, Scott gave in and climbed the steps into the small plane, followed by Garcia, the twins and Mr Delgado. Scott watched the pilot close the door as the guards outside wandered back towards the terminal building.

'Make yourself comfortable, Mr Miller. We have a couple of hours' flight before we reach our destination.'

'What do you want with me?' Scott said to Delgado.

'When we get there, Mr Miller. I will reveal all when we get there.'

The propellers wound up to speed, making a louder, completely different hum to the jet as it taxied to the end of the runway, turned and powered up to takeoff speed. Lifting off the ground over the muddy brown waters of the Guatiquía River, the plane climbed steeply over the lush, green, tree-covered mountain slopes before heading north towards the coast.

Scott sat quietly, looking out the window. The minutes ticked slowly by. Balthasar did most of the talking, his fast Spanish sounding like an angry stream of demands to Scott's uncomprehending ear. Garcia and the twins offered brief responses when called for, their stony-faced expressions rarely changing.

Eventually Scott felt the plane start to descend. He moved closer to the small window, straining to see where they were going. The densely tree-covered mountains below stretched on for miles until they hit a rocky coastline. Only the occasional cleared plot of land was visible through the trees, with small fields of crops and ramshackle wooden farm huts dotted here and there. The plane flew out over the sea before banking around back towards the land. As it turned, a large white house with ornate railings framing its many terraces and bedroom balconies came into view. It had a large pool out back with beautifully manicured gardens set inside its high-walled perimeter.

A hundred-metre-high communications tower sat surrounded by rows of solar panels on the incline to the rear of the house. Satellite dishes and cellular transmitters were bolted to its triangle shaped framework at various heights, with a radio transmitter perched at the very top. As the plane straightened up, the view changed. Smaller buildings, hangars and a grassy airstrip running along one side of the estate all the way to the cliff's edge came into view. Steps carved into the rock led down the cliff face to a jetty. A speed boat rocked gently on the crystal clear Caribbean Sea. At the top of the airstrip, a well used dirt track snaked its way through the trees, disappearing into the distance with no destination in sight.

The plane came in fast, noisily touching down on the bumpy surface. It pulled to a halt next to the heavy gates to enter the estate. A group of armed security that looked more like soldiers or guerilla freedom fighters than security stood to attention at their boss's arrival. The gates parted as the propellers wound to a halt and the aircraft door opened, letting a wave of hot humid air into the plane. Two golf buggies came out to greet them, a smartly dressed member of Balthasar's house staff driving each one.

'Mr Miller,' Delgado said, gesturing for Scott to sit next to him in the lead buggy.

Scott did as he was directed, squinting as the buggy turned into the setting sun and drove back towards the house. Garcia and the twins rode in the buggy behind them.

'I apologise for the unorthodox manner in which I have brought you here, but I do have a job that requires a man of your talents. A job of great importance to my country. A job that requires the utmost secrecy. Come, I will show you to your room. Please, be comfortable, freshen up and change. I have taken the liberty of acquiring some clothes for your stay,' Delgado said, getting out of the buggy and gesturing for Scott to follow him around the pool and into the house.

The interior was magnificent, with a shiny white marble floor running throughout the white painted rooms. Balthasar led him into a large hall at the centre of the building. Twin staircases swept up either side, framing an enormous chandelier that hung from the ceiling in the centre of the hall. They made their way up to the first floor landing. Scott continued to follow Balthasar down a long corridor to a room at the end. A man with classic Colombian features stood by the door, dressed smartly in black trousers and shoes, with an immaculately pressed white shirt and black tie.

'This is Quinto, Mr Miller. He is at your disposal. We have a well-stocked kitchen. Just tell Quinto what you would like to eat and drink. He will get my chef to prepare it for you and bring it to your room. Now if you will excuse me, I have some urgent business to attend to. Please relax and enjoy your room. We will discuss what is required of you at breakfast tomorrow,' said Balthasar, turning and walking away without waiting for a response from Scott.

'I suppose you're going to lock me in my room now?' Scott said to Quinto.

'I'm sorry, er, no. Sir, you are free to move around the house and walk the grounds.'

'Really, and if I decide to leave?' Scott said, looking him in the eye.

'Please, sir, I would not recommend you do that. There are fifty armed guards on the estate and twenty miles of uninhabited rainforests and mountainous terrain in every direction.'

Tired and deflated, Scott moved into the room, shutting the door in Quinto's face.

ELEVEN

After a six-and-a-half-hour flight, the Latam Airlines plane touched down at Bogotá's El Dorado International Airport. Danny stretched and yawned, feeling fatigued. He realised in the last three days he'd flown from the UK to Australia, to Brazil and now to Colombia, while getting involved in a car chase, a gunfight and a punch-up in a drug den.

'Let's find the nearest hotel. I need some sleep and a clear head before I can find Scott.'

'Ok,' Nikki said, looked at his tired face before leaning in and kissing him.

They made their way through customs and baggage claim before grabbing a taxi outside the airport. Danny asked the driver to take them to the nearest decent hotel. The taxi driver took them to a Hyatt hotel a few miles from the airport. Danny checked them into a room on the fourth floor. Too tired to take the stairs, he reluctantly took the lift to the fourth floor. The hands on his watch ticked past midnight as he shut the door behind him. The UK was five hours ahead of Colombia, making it only 5 a.m. He texted Edward.

Got in late. I'll call you when I get up, early p.m. your end.

To his surprise the phone started ringing before he had a chance to throw it on the bed.

'Edward, don't you ever sleep?'

'Very rarely these days, a sign of the times, I'm afraid. Too many bad guys, not enough good ones,' said Edward, still staring at his computer terminal from behind his desk at the Secret Intelligence Service building overlooking the Thames.

'Yeah, I know the feeling. What have you got for me?'

'You sure you want to know?'

'That bad then, go on, let's hear it,' said Danny with a big sigh, followed by a half-hearted smile to reassure Nikki looking at him from the ensuite bathroom.

'Right, well, I called General Dale Parnell. Remember him from the Marcus Tenby saga? Anyway, General Parnell's new department works closely with the CIA and the DEA.'

'Sorry, Edward, I'm knackered. Is this going somewhere?' Danny said, starting to lose his train of thought.

'Sorry, yes. The DEA has an office inside the US Embassy in Bogotá. General Parnell has arranged for your clearance and full co-operation. If you go there tomorrow and ask for DEA Agent Gabriel Anderson, he will assist you in any way he can.'

'That's great, thanks, Edward. What else did you find out?'

'Your Balthasar, El Diablo chap is one Balthasar Delgado, one-time leader of the largest, most ruthless drug cartel in the world. His nickname, El Diablo, was earned from the terrible torture and killings he administered on anyone who crossed him. The DEA agent should be able to tell you more, but from my initial findings, Balthasar Delgado apparently turned his back on the drugs trade some six years ago. He's a born-again good guy—charity work, rehab centres—while working his way up the political ladder. So much so, he's running for President despite rumours of intimidation and vote buying.'

'Sounds like a charmer. What do you reckon they want with Scott?'

'It's got to be something to do with computers. Apart from fast cars and dating supermodels, what else has Scott got?' Edward said, managing a chuckle.

'Yeah, true. Thanks, Edward, I appreciate this,' Danny said, smiling at the thought of Scott's lifestyle.

'Anytime, keep me informed.'

Danny hung up and scratched his unruly mop of hair, yawning.

'Did you find out anything?'

'Quite a bit actually.'

'Well?' Nikki said impatiently.

Danny considered sugar-coating what he'd learned, but thought that never seemed to work well for him in the past, so he told the truth.

Nikki sat on the bed and listened until he'd finished.

'Can you get him back?' she said after a long silence.

'If I can find out where he is. People like that never expect someone to stand up against them. They'll be more worried about Scott getting out than me getting in.'

'It'll be dangerous, you could be killed,' she said, not in panic, but calm as she remembered how Danny dealt with Theodore Blazer's men in Australia.

'A lot of people have tried. I'm still here,' Danny said with a small smile.

'Then do it, get my brother back and kill anyone that gets in your way,' she said, with her eyes fixed on his.

'Yes, ma'am, first thing in the morning. But now I need some sleep.'

They got ready for bed. Danny was asleep within minutes while Nikki lay next to him, her arm across his chest as she looked into the dark hotel room, her mind turning endlessly over possible outcomes. Some good, some bad.

TWELVE

There was a knock on the door at 7:30 a.m. Quinto entered a couple of seconds later.

'Breakfast will be on the pool terrace in half an hour, Mr Miller. Mr Delgado has requested your presence.'

Scott rolled over and watched him leave without saying a word. His head was fuzzy, he'd only managed to get a couple of hours' sleep with his mind doing overtime thinking about his predicament. He looked into the wardrobe full of clothes and picked a cream coloured light linen suit, with a crisp white shirt and navy blue tie.

Just because one is held captive by some sort of mad Colombian gangster, it's no reason for one to let personal standards drop.

Scott tied the perfect Windsor knot, checking the length of his tie was correct before leaving the room to make his way down one of the twin staircases to the hall. He wandered outside and headed for a large table on the pool terrace. The twins, Rico and Felipe, were dressed in expensive suits and watched him through dark sunglasses as they stood motionless by the house.

'Mr Miller, come, sit down,' said Delgado loudly from the head of the table, his arm shooting up as he clicked his fingers at the house staff to pull a chair out for Scott. 'Please, you are my guest. Have anything you want.'

'What I would really like is to know what this is all about,' Scott said, holding Delgado's intense stare.

Leaning over to his left, Delgado whispered something into Garcia's ear. Nodding, Garcia rose from the table and disappeared into the house.

'Let me tell you a little story, Mr Miller. My family were farmers, right here on this very spot, when this was just a few shacks. They grew corn, sugar cane, some livestock. They were very poor. When I took over from my father in the swinging sixties, the USA had just got a taste for marijuana. I saw an opportunity. It grew well in our climate, and back then it was easy to fly it over the border into America.

'The sixties moved into the seventies and America discovered cocaine. We processed it right here, tonnes of it at a cost of $1,500 per kilo, it sold on the streets of America for $50,000 a kilo. I ran the most powerful organisation in the world, thousands of people on the payroll, police, senators, the FBI and the DEA, I ran them all. Then little by little, technology made the business harder, the FBI tapped my phones, scanners listened to my mobile phone conversations, satellites watched us from space as we filled the hangars by the airfield with so much cash we didn't know what to do with it. Anyway, we evolved, learned to be more cautious. The cash went electronic and the drugs went underground.

'Someday in the not too distant future it will be all gone. They will synthesise cocaine to make it too cheap to bother with, or legalise it in some form or other like marijuana and process it in the US under license. It is of no consequence, that is all far behind me. It no longer gives me what I want,' Delgado said, pausing to look up to the skies as if he could see the satellites looking back at him from space.

'And what is it you want?' Scott said, bringing Delgado's train of thought back into focus.

'Power, Mr Miller, I want to run Colombia. The Presidential elections are next week and, despite my considerable influence, there are certain individuals who continue to resist my influence and campaign against me. The polls put me behind the current President Alejandro Perez, making him the favourite for re-election. This is where you come in, Mr Miller. Please, if you will follow me,' Delgado said, getting up from the table.

Scott followed, fully aware of the twins falling in a few paces behind him. Delgado walked to a room at the far corner of the house. Garcia was standing outside and opened the door as they arrived. He stepped back to let Scott see inside. A small, frail looking Colombian man spun around in his chair and looked back at Scott through small round glasses. Several computer terminals sat between an array of monitors on the desks behind him, cables snaking out the back of them to a large data cabinet in the corner. Scott looked out the window past it, his eyes working their way up the communications tower to a large VSAT internet satellite dish fixed halfway up.

'I see you are admiring our communications tower, Mr Miller. We have gigabit internet and a point-to-point cellular link from Santa Marta so I can use my phone. The transmitter at the top is so I can keep in contact with the workers on my land. It's good for about ten miles in every direction, depending on the mountains and valleys,' Delgado boasted.

'Scott Miller, you're him, Scott Miller?' the little man said in surprise.

'This is Luis Rojas. According to Luis, you are the best in the business, which is why you are here. Luis has continually failed to crack the government's AES 256-bit encryption protecting the electoral program. I need you to hack the system and manipulate the results of the votes as they come in from the voting stations and online voters. Can you do it?'

'Mmm, I should think so.'

'By next Friday?' Delgado added coldly.

'Friday! I'm not sure, possibly.'

Delgado nodded to Garcia. He pulled a phone out of his pocket and showed Scott a picture of Nikki and Danny as they exited the airport in Bogotá last night.

'"Possibly' is not the response I want to hear, Mr Miller. My people are everywhere. One phone call and your sister and her troublesome boyfriend are dead. So, I ask you again, can you do it?'

Scott's heart sunk. He knew Delgado would never let him go free, but he had to protect Nikki and Danny. At least he knew Danny had followed his trail to Bogotá.

Just do as Delgado says and buy Danny enough time to find me and get me out of here.

'Yes, I can do it.'

'Good, do as I ask and I will fly you back to Rio with a suitcase containing two million dollars for your inconvenience and discretion.'

Hmm, I don't believe that for a minute.

'Diego, remove Mr Rojas. We don't need him any longer,' Delgado said calmly.

Garcia grabbed Luis roughly by the arm and dragged him up out of his seat. By the terrified look on his face, Scott was under no illusion that something very bad was about to happen to Luis.

'Wait, don't—I—I need him. It'll take both of us to hack the encryption. I can't do it on my own. Not in the timeframe you need it done,' said Scott in a panic.

Delgado looked directly at Scott, trying to figure out if he was being played or not. The seconds ticked by excruciatingly slowly. 'Very well. I have business to attend to in Bogotá. I'll expect a full progress report on my return,' he finally said before turning and leaving the room.

Garcia followed Delgado without saying a word, leaving Luis shaking with beads of sweat on his forehead.

'Are you alright, old man?' Scott said, taking a seat beside Luis.

'Thank you, I'm so sorry I got you involved. I never

thought he'd actually get you here,' Luis said, dabbing his face with a tissue.

'It's alright, my dear fellow, it's not your fault. Now why don't you show me what you've been up to?'

THIRTEEN

Danny woke early, refreshed and clear headed, after eight hours of uninterrupted sleep. After a breakfast of coffee and croissants, they were going to take a taxi to the US Embassy until the receptionist told them it was only half a mile down the road. They walked out into bright sunshine and a pleasant twenty degree heat.

The road was modern and wide, with two lanes of traffic bustling along in either direction. Shops, takeaways and small businesses lined either side, with apartment blocks and a generous selection of hotels dotted in between to serve a continuous supply of travellers to and from the airport.

Following at a discreet distance, two of Balthasar's men kept pace with Danny and Nikki around thirty metres back. They didn't register on Danny's radar until he and Nikki turned off the main road by a park and parade of shops, heading towards the US Embassy as instructed by the receptionist at the Hyatt. Danny caught a glimpse of the two men in the reflection of a delivery lorry's front windscreen. Something in the way they walked put him on edge, upright, striding with purpose, heads up and eyes locked on the back of Danny and Nikki's heads. Careful not to alert Nikki, Danny continued to walk casually along, waiting for the opportunity to get a better view of the men from the reflection in a shop window a little further along the road.

They were definitely following them. Their stride was still too deliberate, too purposeful, their heads never looking around as they stared at their targets. He didn't tell Nikki. They were safe for now. It was daytime, and the street had plenty of people going about their business. If they'd wanted to kill them, a drive-by shooting as they walked out of the hotel would have been an easier choice.

The US Embassy wasn't hard to find, set back from the road with a high wall and heavy metal gates surrounding an imposing white building topped with satellite dishes and antennas. They entered the reception building by the gate and noticed large United States Embassy lettering carved into a stone feature wall. While the woman on reception phoned through to DEA Agent Gabriel Anderson, Danny looked out the black privacy glass at the road outside. He took his phone out of his pocket as the two men who'd been following them walked into view, their heads turning his way to stare at the reception building as they passed by. He doubted they could see him behind the tinted glass, and zoomed in on their faces to take a picture.

'What are you doing?' said Nikki, looking over at him.

'Just taking some holiday snaps,' he said, still watching the two men as they casually walked past the embassy out of sight.

'If you'd like to head across to the main building, Agent Anderson will meet you there,' said the receptionist, handing them their passports and visitors passes back across the desk.

They walked across the car park within the security wall and entered the building's main entrance. A tall, sandy-haired man with a moustache, cheap suit and an overworked, underpaid look about him smiled and headed in their direction.

'Mr Pearson, Miss Miller. Gabriel Anderson, DEA, pleased to meet you,' he said, extending his hand.

Danny and Nikki shook it before following him along the corridors to his small office.

'Please take a seat,' he said, picking a stack of files off one of the visitors' chairs. He turned to put the pile on the desk, but as that was already stacked high, he turned and found a space on top of the filing cabinet.

'You have some friends in very high places, Mr Pearson. General Dale Parnell woke me up at three o'clock this morning, ordering me to assist you in anyway I can. So, how can I assist you?' Gabriel said with a tired smile.

'What can you tell us about Balthasar Delgado, also known as El Diablo?' Danny said, getting straight to the point.

'El Diablo, I haven't heard him called that in a while.

Er, right, hang on a minute.'

Gabriel moved a stack of files off his desk and put them on the floor before walking to a filing cabinet. He pulled the drawer open and riffled through it before pulling a fat file out and placing it on the desk.

'Our job in Colombia is to gather information and collect evidence we can use in a US court. Any actionable information about crimes committed in Colombia is shared with the Colombian National Police and the Colombian Prosecutor's office. Now, six years ago we were close to getting Balthasar Delgado. We had undercover DEA agents in his organisation Stateside, a top-level informant in Colombia, and satellite images of the cocaine being brought into and flying out of his family estate in the Pico mountains near Santa Marta on the Caribbean coast. Then it all went to hell. They butchered the undercover agents in the US. Delgado's Stateside distribution network went underground, and the informant was found hanging from a church tower with his throat slit and his heart cut out as a warning to others. The Colombian National Police raided Delgado's house here in Bogotá and his family estate in the Pico mountains and found nothing. Case closed.'

'So that's it then, he cleaned up his act and went into politics,' said Nikki.

'Not exactly. The supply of drugs into the States never stopped. Delgado, or rather El Diablo's name, is still mentioned in the criminal underworld. We just don't know how he's getting it out of the country. Satellite imagery shows no planes, no boats leaving his estate on the Caribbean coast. We occasionally find and burn a coca plantation or cocaine processing plant in the remote forest regions that surround his estate, but we have no proof that it's his, and nobody will talk. It would be like signing their own death warrant,' Gabriel said, handing Danny satellite images of Delgado's estate and house in Bogotá.

'Can I have copies of these and the addresses?'

'Of course, General Parnell has given you full clearance. But may I ask what your interest in Balthasar Delgado is?'

'He kidnapped my friend, Scott Miller in Rio de Janeiro and flew him to Bogotá on a private jet,' Danny said, still studying the satellite images.

'That's not Delgado's usual M.O. Shootings, revenge killings, bribery and intimidation are more his style, not kidnapping. Do you have any idea why he would kidnap your friend?'

'It's obviously not money. Scott's pretty well off, but it's nothing compared to Delgado. He'd make more than Scott has with one shipment of cocaine. The only other thing is computers. Scott Miller is a world-renowned computer expert,' Danny said, stopping when he noticed Gabriel sit up at the mention of computers. 'What is it?'

'Er, hang on, it's here somewhere,' Gabriel said, frantically moving files around as he searched for something. 'Ah, here it is.'

Gabriel handed a copy of The City Paper, an English language newspaper, to Danny.

'Bogotá shocked by macabre gang murders?' Danny

said, looking up puzzled.

'No, no, the story under that,' Gabriel said, pointing further down the page.

'Senior government IT consultant and his wife go missing?'

'Yes, that one.'

'IT consultant Luis Rojas and his wife Tia Rojas were reported missing last Tuesday evening after their car was found abandoned a mile from their home in Rosales. Mr Rojas, the CEO of Kincade Computer Systems, and his wife disappeared whilst on their way to a party hosted by President Alejandro Perez.'

'Quite a coincidence, don't you think? That's last week's paper, so he's been missing for ten days.'

'Yes it is,' Danny said, looking at the picture of Mr and Mrs Rojas in the paper.

'Do you have anything to link Delgado with your friend's disappearance? I can help you liaise with the police, but I will need some evidence for them to open an investigation, especially as the abduction of your friend took place in another country.'

'No, the man who told me that Scott had been brought here is dead,' said Danny matter-of-fact.

'I see, then I'm not sure what more I can do,' Gabriel said, looking apologetically towards Nikki as her face sank.

'It's ok, you've been very helpful. If I can just have those copies, we'll be on our way.'

'Of course,' Gabriel got up and took the papers to the photocopier in the office outside. 'Here, take my card.

Call me if you find anything I can take to the authorities.'

Danny took the copies and Gabriel's business card, then he and Nikki followed him back to reception.

'Good luck, Mr Pearson, Miss Miller. I hope you find your friend,' Gabriel said, shaking their hands.

'Thank you,' Nikki said, while Danny just gave him a nod.

'Oh and Mr Pearson, Balthasar Delgado might want us to think he's cleaned up his act, but he's a very powerful and dangerous man. He has people everywhere. Be very careful.'

'I always am,' Danny said, taking Nikki's hand as they left the embassy.

FOURTEEN

'So what do we do now?' said Nikki on the street outside the embassy.

'The second thing I'm going to do is rent a car so I can go take a look at Delgado's Bogotá house,' Danny said, his eyes flicking around without moving his head, scanning the street before checking reflections in windows and vehicles to see what was behind them.

'What's the first thing?' said Nikki, looking up at him.

'You see that street up ahead on your right, by the gardener standing next to his pickup truck?'

'Yes, I see it.'

'We're going to turn down there, then you're going to continue to walk for forty paces and turn and wait for the two guys following us to catch up to you.'

'Wait, what? We're being followed?'

'Yep, don't turn around. Just do what I said, honey. Everything will be fine. OK,' Danny said, catching another glimpse of the two men following in a shop window.

'And what are you going to do?'

'Oh, just a little digging,' Danny said with a smile.

They turned the corner. The second they were out of sight of their followers, masked by the house on the corner, Danny peeled off, vanishing around the front of a parked minivan. He crouched down and moved along the roadside towards the rear of the minivan before scooting across the gap to bob down behind the gardener's pickup truck. As the two men walked by on the kerbside, Danny moved to the rear of the pickup, carefully sliding his arm into the back to pick something up. The two men took a few steps before stopping, surprised at Nikki turning to face them, confused at the disappearance of Danny. Before they could react, there was a metallic thwacking noise and one dropped to the pavement out cold. The other turned just in time to see the shovel Danny had lifted out of the gardener's pickup heading for his face. There was another loud metallic thwack before the second man joined his buddy on the floor.

Danny bobbed down on his haunches and patted them both down, reaching inside their jackets to remove handguns from their shoulder holsters. He tucked one into the back of his jeans before kneeling on the chest of the guy he'd hit in the face. His front teeth were missing and Danny had broken his nose, but with a few slaps on the side of his face he started to come round.

'You speak English?' Danny growled, pushing the barrel of the gun against his forehead.

The guy's eyes just narrowed as he stared back

defiantly.

'Ok, your choice, buddy,' Danny said, cocking the slide on the Glock to chamber a bullet ready to fire.

The guy's eyes widened and centred on Danny's finger as it flexed on the trigger, flicking up in panic to plead with Danny's darkening face.

'Ok, ok,' he blurted out quickly.

'Where's Scott Miller?'

'What?'

'Where is Scott Miller?' Danny repeated slowly, pushing the barrel of the gun harder into the man's forehead.

'I don't know any Miller. We were just told to follow you and report back.'

'Report back to who?'

'Diego Garcia,' the guy said quickly as Danny's finger reapplied pressure on the trigger.

'Who's he?'

'Mr Delgado's right hand man.'

Danny got off the man and beckoned Nikki over while tucking the gun in the back of the jeans with the other one, taking care to cover them with his jacket.

'Don't follow us,' Danny growled, picking up the shovel in one hand and taking Nikki's hand in the other. 'Gracias amigos,' he said, smiling as he handed the shovel back to the watching gardener standing shocked, rake in hand on the lawn of the house on the corner.

'Ok, that wasn't scary at all. I guess we're onto the second thing now,' Nikki said, trying to make light of things.

'No, that was just an impromptu reaction. The first thing we're going to do is check out of the hotel and put you on a plane out of Colombia,' Danny said, checking behind them to make sure the men weren't following

'No, I want to help,' she said, pulling him to a stop.

'I know you do, but what just happened back there was nothing. This is going to get a hell of a lot more dangerous than that. I can't beat these guys and find Scott if I have to protect you at the same time.'

She held back the urge to protest, looking at him for a long time until she finally nodded her agreement.

'Good, let's get checked out of the hotel and I'll get you on the very next flight out of Colombia.'

They checked out and took a taxi to the airport. After queuing at three different flight desks, they finally found one with space on a flight to Jamaica in a couple of hours' time.

'Book yourself into a good hotel. I'll call you as soon as I find where Scott is,' Danny said.

'I was going to say be careful, but I know you always are. Just get my brother and come back to me, ok?'

Danny just nodded and kissed her again before leaving her at the boarding gate to head for the Alamo car rental desk. Twenty minutes later he was following the sat nav on his phone as he drove into the hills on the outskirts of Bogotá.

The houses got larger and further apart the higher he climbed up the steep slopes, lush green forest filling the gaps between them. Seeing Delgado's large modern house up ahead, Danny drove past the high wall and large electric gates to park up in a lay-by half a mile further up the hill. He got out, but instead of heading back down the road, he disappeared into the treeline, heading up the slope for thirty metres before turning and tacking parallel to the road towards Delgado's house. It took him ten minutes to negotiate the dense undergrowth before coming out along the side of the property's surrounding wall. With a small run up, Danny dug the toe of his trainer into the rough render halfway up the wall, giving him enough grip to push down and get his fingertips over the top edge. He pulled himself up slowly until he could see over.

A long brickweave drive ran along the side of the wall below him. It ran along the length of the property to a large parking area near the swimming pool to the rear of the house. There were two cars parked on it, an old Hyundai and a shiny new Toyota 4x4. Danny guessed the old Hyundai would belong to some sort of domestic staff. Ignoring his muscles as they burned from holding his position, Danny turned his head towards the front gate. A guy wandered close to it, short and stocky, dressed in jeans and a shirt with a handgun sitting in a holster on his belt. He looked bored as he smoked a cigarette.

There was a shout from somewhere to the front of the house. The guy looked up and nodded to someone before walking in their direction, disappearing around the corner out of sight. Danny pulled himself up to sit on top of the wall, as his shoulders and arms enjoyed the relief. A clicking sound made him look over the wall at the ground directly below him. A guard like the one on the gate leaned against the wall below, lighting a cigarette with a Zippo lighter. Moving slowly, Danny swung his feet up and silently moved up into a crouching position. He checked no one else was around, then looked down at the top of the guard's head.

This is a really bad idea. One, two, three

FIFTEEN

'It can't be done. I've been trying for over a week and got nowhere. The AES encryption cannot be hacked with any kind of key generation decryption program,' said Luis, slumping back in his seat.

'My dear boy, there's a saying we have in England. There's more than one way to skin a cat,' Scott said, tapping away at the keyboard while looking intently between three different screens.

'Eh, what has skinning a cat got to do with anything?'

'It just means there's more than one way to look at the problem in hand.'

'How? There's only one way in, and that's generating a key to unlock the encryption,' Luis said, rubbing his forehead as he tried to relieve his headache.

'Are you alright, old man?'

'I'm just worried about my wife.'

'Where is she?' Scott stopped typing to look at him.

'I don't know. They're keeping her somewhere else, Bogotá, I think. Delgado puts her on the phone when he's away from here to make me work harder. He offered me the same deal as you, two million when it's done and my wife and I go free. He's going to kill us all as soon as he gets what he wants. You know that, right?'

'Yes, old man, I suspect as much, but I still have a few tricks up my sleeve. Come on, let's take a break, grab a coffee and have a walk around the gardens,' Scott said with a smile.

Luis sighed and followed Scott out of the room. Quinto appeared out of nowhere before they got to the kitchen.

'Can I get you anything?'

'Yes, a coffee would be very nice, Quinto. I'll take it on the pool terrace, and you, Luis?'

'Yes, coffee for me too,' Luis said, looking nervously from behind Scott.

'I'll bring it out to you,' said Quinto, his eyes flicking to look behind them both, and then flicking back before he smiled and headed off towards the kitchen.

Scott turned to see what Quinto had looked at. One of the twins emerged from a door under the left staircase. Scott ignored the intimidating stare, taking in the stairs that led down below ground level behind him. Noticing Scott's gaze, he slammed the door shut and stood in front of it, pulling his suit jacket to one side to display the holstered gun underneath.

'Good morning,' Scott said, smiling as he walked casually past him towards the pool terrace with Luis trying to look invisible as he followed along behind him.

Out in the bright sunshine, Scott and Luis sat in

silence until Quinto brought the coffee. He placed the drinks on the table before leaving them.

Out of the corner of his eye, Scott noticed the twins emerging from the house to stand motionless by the large sliding doors, watching him through their wraparound shades.

'Shall we take a walk?' Scott said, flicking his eyes in their direction before picking his cup up and strolling casually around the pool.

Taking Scott's hint, Luis followed him out of the twins' earshot, catching up with him by the steps leading down to the lawn.

'What a charming pair they are,' Scott muttered.

'Be careful of the twins, Rico and Felipe. Delgado's men brought a woman here last week. They said she had been stealing from him. One word from Delgado and Rico put a bullet in her head,' said Luis, still walking nervously beside Scott.

'That might be so, old man, but until we give Delgado what he wants, they can't touch us.'

'How does this help us? We fail, they kill us; we succeed, they kill us.'

'Time, my dear boy. It buys us time,' Scott said, turning his head at the sound of a truck approaching through the rainforest.

Looking back at the house, Scott noticed Rico talking on a radio. When he turned back to the sound of the approaching truck, he spotted a guard talking into another radio handset as he looked in Rico's direction. The guard nodded and headed to the hangar on the airfield, pulling the large door open before standing to one side.

'Time. Time for what?' Luis said, moving in front of Scott to stop him.

'Time for someone to find us,' Scott said, watching the truck appear on the other side of the wall. It drove along the side of the airstrip before disappearing through the open hangar door. The guard pulled the door shut behind it.

'Find us? How's anyone going to find us out here?' Luis said, looking totally disheartened.

'My dear Luis, I didn't say anyone, I said someone. Someone who is particularly good at finding people. Now, I wonder what's going on in there,' Scott said, more interested in the truck than Luis.

'You're crazy. Who cares about the trucks? The trucks don't help us get out of here. They come and go all the time. They disappear into the hangar, forty minutes later they come out and disappear back into the rainforest. You want to know what's weird? They drive in forwards and when they come out they are facing the opposite direction. How is that possible? That hangar isn't wide enough to turn a truck around in.'

'Mmm, how very stranger' Scott said, drinking the last of his coffee.

'So how do we break the AES encryption and gain access to the system?' Luis said, trying to shake off his feeling of dread by focusing on the problem in hand.

'The electoral roll program is only one part of a server system that feeds a multitude of national services, military, police, the government itself, these being protected with the highest AES encryption. What you've been overlooking, my dear fellow, is the lesser protected systems, the libraries and schools, hospitals and pharmacies, et cetera. They all link to a national database which is held on the same server as the government's electoral roll program. Instead of trying to find the key to unlock the main server, we find a way into one of the lesser protected systems and change the lock to fit our own key. To work, old chap, we might as well keep ourselves busy while we wait,' Scott said with a smile, heading back towards the house.

Luis followed Scott as he put the coffee cup down on the table and walked around the pool to the house.

'Excuse me, gentlemen,' Scott said, deliberately antagonising the twins to make them move so he could go inside.

Ignoring their scowls, Scott headed for the computer room. He paused in thought for a moment in the hall, looking at the door under the stairs before marching off down the corridor. He entered the computer room, took his seat at the computer, and started typing furiously on the keyboard.

SIXTEEN

Danny stood before dropping off the wall. With one leg bent, he aimed his knee at the point where the neck joined between the guard's shoulder blades. It struck the man like being hit by a sledgehammer, the blow flattening him onto his chest before the full falling weight of Danny crushed him into the ground, blowing the air out of his lungs. Before he could draw breath and think through the shock of what had happened, Danny cracked him on the temple repeatedly with the butt of the handgun he'd gotten from Delgado's men earlier. When the guard went limp, Danny stayed crouched and scanned the grounds for alerted guards. The guard patrolling the front was still out of sight, and he couldn't see anyone looking out from the house. Grabbing the unconscious guard's leg, Danny dragged him across the drive and into a patch of well-manicured bushes and plants next to the house, tucking him under the foliage and out of sight.

Now to find a way in.

The best way to describe the house was a modern design with two floors of boxed shapes stacked with parts overhanging other parts, so the upstairs balconies of the glass, panoramic-viewed bedroom windows overhung the downstairs living areas. Danny headed towards the rear of the property, darting his head around each brick section to get a quick look through the downstairs windows. Checking the coast was clear before moving swiftly to the next bricked section of wall, he reached the rear door leading into a large open plan living and kitchen area with by-folding doors to the outside pool terrace. With a gun in one hand, Danny pushed the handle down slowly and eased the door open, his eyes sweeping the area ahead of him before he slid inside. Rolling his feet from heel to toe, he moved silently across the kitchen, his gun outstretched, his aim locked onto his line of sight. As he reached a door at the far end of the kitchen, Danny could hear some movement on the other side.

This is still a really bad idea. One, two, three.

In one movement, he pushed the door open a couple of feet, the gun sweeping in ahead of him, much to the surprise of an old woman doing the washing in the utility room looked back at him. Her eyes went wide at the sight of the gun and she crossed herself religiously while rambling something in Spanish. Danny put his palm up to quiet her, then held a finger to his lips. She nodded to show she understood.

'*Quédate*,' Danny managed to say. He wanted to add stay here quietly but could only remember the Spanish for stay.

Backing out and closing the door behind him, Danny prayed the old woman stayed silent as he headed for the hall. He stopped outside and listened to the silence beyond before entering. Knowing he was pushing his luck, Danny continued to move fast, sweeping the rooms downstairs, his gun covering every inch as it moved in sync with his eyeline. The rooms were empty, but as he looked out the front through the windows, he could see the guard that had been by the gate standing with two more armed men.

Better make this quick, Danny boy, you're on borrowed time.

Heading up the stairs, Danny checked two bedrooms, both empty. He tried the door of a third room and found it locked. When he put his ear to the door, he could hear someone moving around inside.

'Scott, is that you?' he said as loud as he dared.

Before any answer came back, the door to the bathroom opposite opened. A thickset Colombian man appeared, wiping his hands on his jeans after rinsing them in the sink. He froze, locked in a moment of surprise. Danny didn't freeze. He shoved his gun in the guy's face and pushed him back into the bathroom, reaching forward with his free hand to relieve the man of the gun tucked in his shoulder holster.

'Down on your knees,' Danny growled.

The guy didn't move, just looked at him like a man who'd had a gun in his face before. Danny turned him around and kicked him in the back of the legs behind the knee joint. His legs gave way, and he went down on his front. Putting the gun on the edge of the sink, Danny undid the man's belt and pulled his hands behind his back, tying them together tight. Kneeling on the guy's back, Danny grabbed the towels off a shelf and ripped them into strips. He quickly tied the ankles together before hogtying the man, with his ankles tied to his wrists behind his back. Picking the gun off the sink, Danny stuck the barrel in the guy's side.

'Open, er, fuck, *abi* something. *Abierto*,' Danny said, giving him a slap on the side of the face while miming for him to open his mouth.

When he did, Danny stuffed a wedge of towel in and tied another strip around his head to gag him. Patting the guy down, Danny found some keys and assumed they were for the door across the hall. Shutting the bathroom door behind him, Danny moved across the hall, unlocked the door and pushed it open.

'Scott?'

Instead of Scott, a slim Colombian woman stared back at him.

'Shit. Come. Er, we go. Er, you're free. *Vamos*, ok?' Danny said, turning to leave, downhearted.

'You're looking for Scott Miller, yes?' the woman said to his surprise.

'Yes, do you know where he is?'

'He is with my husband. Delgado has them at his estate in the Pico mountains on the Caribbean coast.'

'He kidnapped you as well?'

'Yes, to make my husband do as he says,' the woman said, nervous at what she should do next.

'What's your name?' Danny said, giving her a smile to relax her.

'Tia, Tia Rojas, my husband is Luis Rojas.'

'Ok Tia. One thing at a time. First, let's get you out of here, then I can take you to the police station.'

'No, no, you can't. The police work for Delgado. It was the police who stopped our car near where we live. It was the police who took us to Delgado,' Tia said, a look of dread on her face.

'Shit, ok, ok. Then we'll go to the coast and get your husband and Scott back.'

A look of hope and relief washed across Tia's face as Danny extended his hand for her to hold. With his gun up in the other hand, Danny led her back down the stairs and out the back door. He took a quick look towards the front gate. The coast was clear so he led her swiftly across the drive to the wall. Throwing his back against it, he tucked the gun into his belt and linked his fingers together for her to put her foot in. As she did, he pushed her up the wall until her body leaned over the top edge. As soon as she swung over and dropped down the other side, Danny took a few steps back, ran and jumped up at the wall, pulling himself up and over to drop down the other side next to Tia.

'Ok, this way, quickly, we don't have much time before they find the guard.'

Instead of fighting their way through the dense undergrowth for the half mile back to the car, Danny risked coming out onto the road after a hundred yards and running the rest of the way at Tia's pace, which was surprisingly fast.

'Thank you,' Tia said, shutting the passenger door before Danny drove away up the steep slope.

Danny just nodded back with a reassuring smile.

SEVENTEEN

The large electric gates slid back to let the three car procession drive in. Balthasar Delgado and Diego Garcia got out of the lead car, their eyes staring unnervingly at the guards standing around the guard Danny had jumped on from the wall. He was sitting on the front steps holding a cool, wet towel to the side of his temple. Eight tough-looking men in suits got out of the following two cars. They stood a little way back from Delgado and Garcia, a slight bulge under each jacket from their handguns nestled in shoulder holsters.

'What happened here?' Delgado demanded, noticing the apprehension for any of them to speak first.

'Someone jumped Roberto near the rear of the house.'

'Did you see who it was?'

Roberto looked up at him and shook his head. By the looks on their faces, Delgado could tell there was more to come.

'What else?' he shouted, his temper rising fast.

'He got into the house, tied Arvin up at gunpoint and took the woman.'

'What? And where were you three idiots when this happened?' Delgado growled menacingly, his face moving within inches of his nervous employee.

'We were guarding the front gate, Mr Delgado. He must have come over the wall.'

'Oh really, you only have one job, you incompetent idiot. I pay you to guard, that's it, just guard, and you can't even do that right. Where's Arvin?'

'He's in the kitchen, sir.'

'Diego,' Delgado summoned, walking away from the four men towards the entrance to the house. He stopped just before entering and turned towards the eight men he'd arrived with. 'Kill them. They are of no use to me.'

Delgado turned and went inside.

'No, no, please.'

'No, Señor Delgado.'

Delgado didn't flinch as gunfire rang out behind him. He walked through the house into the large kitchen, where Arvin quickly got up off a stool and stood to attention by the breakfast bar.

'What happened, Arvin?' Delgado said, his anger a little more in check.

'He just appeared. Stuck a gun in my face and tied me up before taking the Rojas woman. There was nothing I could do.'

'Did you recognise him?'

'Yes, it was the Englishman, Scott Miller's friend. The one I photographed with his sister at the airport, the one who got the drop on our two men in Bogotá this morning.'

'The troublesome boyfriend again,' Delgado said, pacing up and down the kitchen, deep in thought. 'Arvin, pack a bag. My contact at the airport said Nikki Miller took a flight to Jamaica this morning. Take Roberto and find her.'

'Do you want me to kill her?'

'No, just call me when you've found her. She's more useful alive for the moment.'

'Yes sir,' Arvin said leaving the room, pleased to be off the hook for losing Tia Rojas.

'What about the boyfriend, this Pearson man? He will go to the police, yes? Do you want me to call the Jozano?' Garcia said once Arvin was out of earshot.

Delgado stood and thought for a while before finally speaking. 'No, this man, Pearson, whoever he is, or was, he is not the sort of man who will go to the police. Also, I used Jozano's men to pick up Luis Rojas and his wife, so she will not want to go there. No, she is with him and she knows where her husband and Miller are. They will try to get a flight to Santa Marta. Phone the airports. If they try to fly from Bogotá, we'll have them detained. If they fly from La Vanguardia Airport, make sure they get on one of our planes. Tell the twins to expect more guests.'

'Do you want me to cancel your engagements and arrange the flight back to your estate?'

'No, I have to keep up with the electoral campaign. We have a hospital visit this afternoon and a school in the morning. We will fly back the day after tomorrow.'

'Ok,' said Diego, getting his phone out to make the necessary arrangements.

EIGHTEEN

Forty minutes outside of Bogotá, Danny realised he hadn't eaten all day and gave in to his grumbling stomach. He pulled in at the next roadside diner and went inside with Tia.

'Here, take a seat, order anything you like,' Danny said, sliding into a booth.

'I'm ok, I'll just have a drink. I don't think I can stomach anything,' she said, still looking nervously around expecting Delgado's men to appear at any moment.

'You should try to eat something.'

'Ok.'

Danny ordered some arepas and empanadas, devouring the lot before ordering seconds. Tia managed to eat a little between glances out the window at every car that passed by or pulled into the diner.

'What does Delgado want with your husband and Scott?' Danny asked after clearing his plate.

'I don't know, something to do with computer

programming and the election.'

'Right. So, any ideas how we get to Delgado's estate in, where was it?'

'It is on a remote part of the coast near the Pico mountains. We will have to fly to the city of Santa Marta. It's the closest airport to the estate.'

'And how close is that?'

'About two hours' drive through dense rainforest.'

'Really, well how does Delgado get in and out?' Danny said half to her, half to himself.

'He flies in and out from his own private airfield,' Tia said straight back.

Danny turned his head away from the window and looked straight at her. 'How do you know so much about Delgado's place?'

'My family are from a village in the rainforest near Santa Marta. We have been living in fear of El Diablo's drug cartel for many years. I met my husband Luis at university and moved away to Bogotá.'

'Do you still have family there?'

'Yes, my uncle, brothers, cousins, a lot of family.'

'Will they help us?'

'Yes, some of them, I'm sure. They are farmers. Delgado forced them off their land to grow his coca plant for cocaine production under the cover of the rainforest.'

'Ok, can we fly from Bogotá?' Danny said, getting his phone out to search for flights.

'Delgado has people at the airport. I think it would be better to get a private charter from La Vanguardia

Airport. It's smaller, about a two hour drive from here.'

Danny looked at his watch. The sun had already gone down and with the drive, they wouldn't get there until late.

'I doubt we'll be able to get a flight tonight. I'll find us a hotel near the airport and we can try to get a flight first thing in the morning.'

They drove all the way to Vanguardia, passing several hotels near the airport until Danny spotted a small, quiet hotel on the outskirts of town. The receptionist looked bored and was happy to take cash and skip the registration cards. Danny was going to book two rooms next to each other when Tia stepped in and asked for a twin room.

'If you don't mind, I don't want to be alone,' she said, hoping he wouldn't object.

Danny gave her a warm smile and said, 'Ok.'

While Tia took a shower, Danny made a video call to Nikki.

'Danny, are you alright? Have you found Scott?' she said, speaking fast.

'Whoa, one thing at a time, love. Yes I'm ok, and yes I know where Scott is. How are you?'

'I'm ok, I miss you.'

'I miss you too,' Danny said just as Tia walked behind him with dripping wet hair and only a towel around her.

'Who the hell is that?' Nikki said, her face dropping.

Danny smiled and chuckled at her. 'That is Tia Rojas, Luis Rojas' wife, the ones that went missing.'

'Yes, I remember who they are, but why is she in a

bedroom with you with no clothes on?'

'I rescued her from Balthasar Delgado's Bogotá mansion. They are holding her husband and Scott at Delgado's country estate on the Caribbean coast. She was too scared to sleep in a room by herself so we got a twin, ok? She was just taking a shower. It's been a long day,' Danny said in a low, calm voice, moving the phone around to show her the twin beds.

'Mmm, ok. But don't you go getting any funny ideas, you hear me?' Nikki said, understanding but still pulling Danny's leg.

'Don't worry, the only funny ideas I have all have you in them.'

Nikki smiled and blushed a little. 'So what's next, the police?'

'No, the police down here are corrupt. We're going to get a flight to Santa Marta tomorrow. Tia has family there that will help us.'

'Ok, just be careful. I want you and my brother back in one piece.'

'That's what I'm aiming for. I'll call you again when I have more news.'

'Ok, I love you,' Nikki said, reluctant to hang up.

'Yeah, I love you too. Don't worry, I'll get him back.'

After they hung up, Danny lay back on the bed. He stared at the ceiling, deep in thought.

'Thank you for helping me and Luis, Mr Pearson,' Tia said, getting into bed.

Danny turned to look at her. He smiled and nodded back before turning the light out, putting his head on the pillow, and shutting his eyes.

NINETEEN

Scott wandered down one of the grand staircases, his eyes drawn to the door underneath the one opposite. He'd seen the twins and several of Delgado's other men coming out of that door and his natural curiosity was killing him. Before he got to the bottom step, Quinto appeared in front of him.

'Can I get you anything, Mr Miller?' he said politely.

'No, no, my good man, I'm just off to fetch a glass of water. I can get it myself,' Scott said with a false smile.

'Very good, sir. There's still or sparkling in the refrigerator.'

'Thank you, Quinto.'

Good heavens, that man sticks to me like a damn leech, doesn't he ever go to bed?

Scott entered the kitchen and got himself a drink. Quinto hovered near the doorway, watching him until he finished his drink and walked past him.

'Right, I'm off to bed, old man. I'll see you in the morning no doubt,' Scott said, walking away.

He took a quick look behind him as he entered the hall, pleased to see Quinto hadn't followed in his shadow. Moving quickly, Scott went to the door under the stairs and tried the handle. The door opened to reveal a lit stone staircase heading down to the basement.

Now, what's so interesting down here that requires so many visitors?

After a quick check to make sure that Quinto or anyone else wasn't watching, Scott stepped inside and closed the door softly behind him. He descended the steps, which opened out into a massive wine cellar.

'Mmm, well, that's a disappointment. Ah, a Château Ausone. Very nice, you can come with me, my dear,' Scott muttered, sliding the bottle out of the rack. He was about to head back up the stairs when he heard a loud creak on the far side of the cellar. Rolling himself around behind the wine rack, Scott backed as far into the shadows as he could. Watching through the gaps between the wine bottles, he watched a section of wall complete with a wine rack attached open outwards, pulled by one of Delgado's guards from the other side. The guard turned and pulled the secret door shut before heading up the basement stairs, oblivious to Scott's watching from the shadows.

Moving back out into the cellar, Scott slid the bottle back into the rack and headed over to take a look. Even standing directly in front of the doorway, it was impossible to see it. He gave it a push but it didn't move. Looking at the bottles in the middle rack, Scott noticed one he'd never heard of. It was also the only bottle in the rack that had no dust on it. When he pulled it forward, he found it had a rod attached to its base. The rod pulled a latch inside the wall and the doorway clicked and popped inwards a couple of inches. Scott pushed it all the way back, a wheel on the bottom of the door squeaking as it rolled across the stone floor. Behind it, a tunnel stretched some fifty or sixty metres away with bulkhead lights fixed to one side at ten metre intervals.

How delightfully intriguing.

Closing the heavy door behind him, Scott headed off down the tunnel as it extended way out past the boundaries of the house, heading in the direction of the sea. The flat tunnel eventually ended in steps, heading down and down through solid rock. As he went deeper, Scott could hear sounds echoing back up the tunnel towards him, people's shouts and engine noise mixed with the sound of lapping water. The steps eventually ended, and the tunnel levelled out with an exit visible up ahead. Scott couldn't believe his eyes when the tunnel came out into a massive underground cave, lit up by powerful floodlights fixed high up on the rock's surface.

At the far end, the cave wall dipped into a massive pool of deep sea water. Streams of sunlight danced and rippled below the surface from the underwater opening to the Caribbean Sea outside. A large dock to Scott's left had been constructed in concrete to accommodate the ex-Russian Yasen-M nuclear submarine that had just surfaced. Water still ran off its surface from the deep water at the bottom of the cave as the hatches opened on top.

Hearing voices, Scott moved out of sight behind a stack of crates on the dock. He peeped between them to see a lorry on the far side. A forklift reversed and turned as it removed the last pallet stacked high with cocaine bricks. It drove along the dock and placed the pallet next to the submarine. A shout made him look back towards the lorry. It moved forward a few metres and stopped. The whine of an electric motor sounded and the lorry started to rotate on a large metal circular plate in the floor. When it faced the opposite direction, the truck drove off up a slope and disappeared out of sight.

To the hangar. Mmm, in one way and out the other. Very clever.

There was more activity on the submarine. Men exited onto its black surface, tying the submarine to mooring posts on the jetty before opening a large cargo hatch at the front. Within minutes a chain of men started passing suitcase-sized bundles of plastic-wrapped dollar bills towards the jetty while the guards stacked bundle after bundle into a neat square pile on an empty pallet.

Mmm, given up drug smuggling my arse, an ingenious way of getting it in and out of the States undetected.

Curiosity satisfied, Scott headed back along the long tunnel to the wine cellar. He pulled the heavy secret door shut behind him, and was about to climb the stairs to the house when he stopped and headed back to the wine rack he'd hidden behind earlier.

'Sorry, my dear, I almost forgot you,' he said, chuckling to himself as he slid the bottle of Château

Ausone out.

He emerged from the cellar to shouts. Rico ran over to him and grabbed him by the throat, pushing him up against the wall.

'What were you doing down there? The cellar is out of bounds. You don't go down there,' he said, his face inches away from Scott's.

'Steady, old man, you wouldn't want to hurt me, would you? Especially as I haven't completed my task for your boss. Mr Delgado said to make myself at home, so I was just fetching a nice little bottle of red for a nightcap. Care to join me?' Scott said with more than a little smugness in his voice.

Rico glared at him, looking fit to explode, but the fear of what his boss would do if he hurt Scott and jeopardised the project far outweighed his own desire to put a bullet in Scott's forehead, so he released him.

'That's better. There's a good boy. Right, I'm off to bed, toodle-oo,' Scott said, heading up the stairs to his room without looking back.

TWENTY

Danny awoke early. The moment he was out of bed Tia opened her eyes in a flash of panic. She relaxed a second later when her brain processed where she was and that she was with the man who'd rescued her.

'You ok? Sorry, stupid question,' Danny said as reassuringly as he could.

'I'm ok,' she said, sitting up.

They got dressed and headed to the hotel's diner. Danny tucked into eggs, bread and some sort of rice, beans and tomatoes mixture, washed down with gallons of coffee. He was glad to see Tia eat some scrambled eggs and bread. When they finished, they drove over to La Vanguardia Airport. Danny stripped the guns, wiping them down in the car before they got out. He discreetly dropped the bullets and slides down a drain before shoving the other components deep into a bin outside the terminal building before they entered. Danny let Tia negotiate for a ticket to Santa Marta. His Spanish sucked and her being a local seemed to get a more helpful response. He stood back as they talked. There was lots of pointing to this desk and that. They moved through four different operators' desks until she managed to get seats on a small cargo plane leaving for Santa Marta in a couple of hours. With nothing else to do, they went through security's metal detector and baggage check and sat in a small, hot, stuffy waiting area.

The hours passed slowly until a guy loosely dressed as a pilot, white shirt with stripes on the shoulders, jeans and flip-flops, beckoned them to follow him across the tarmac to an old Cessna 408 SkyCourier, a twin turboprop small cargo plane from the 1960s, hand-painted in patchy matt green paint.

'Jeez, do you think it'll get off the ground?' Danny muttered as he climbed inside.

'It will. I have faith,' said Tia with a small smile.

The back of the plane was full of crates and boxes, all strapped down securely, leaving just enough room for the six passenger seats behind the pilot's cockpit. Sitting in the rear seats, Danny caught the pilot giving him a strange look through the half-open curtain that separated the cockpit from the main body of the plane. He didn't like it, but put it down to the fact he was probably the first foreigner hitching a ride across Colombia that he'd ever had.

At the last minute, two thickset Colombians climbed on board, the co-pilot closing the door the second they took the seats directly in front of Danny and Tia. The hairs on the back of Danny's neck stood up when he noticed an exchange of looks between all three of them, followed by a flick of their eyes in his direction as the co-pilot returned to the cockpit. The engines fired up and the loud, rattly old plane taxied its way to the runway. Danny watched the back of the heads in front as the engines roared and the plane accelerated to takeoff speed.

Don't be paranoid. Two hours, that's all, just two hours until we land. Nothing's going to happen.

And nothing did happen, not until they felt the plane gently start to descend. Danny caught Tia looking out the window with a worried frown on her face.

'What is it?'

'This is wrong, we've just passed over the Pico mountains and we're already going down for landing. Santa Marta is further along the coast.'

Even over the drone of the engines, Danny heard the familiar metallic sound of a gun slide being pulled back and the click of a bullet entering its chamber. Bending forward, he reached under the seat and ripped the lifejacket out of its storage pouch. As the two men in front got up and turned, Danny darted forward and hooked the life jacket over the nearest guy's head and yanked it down hard. He pulled the guy's chin onto the headrest, holding it there with one hand before punching him as hard as he could in the face with the other. As his head flew backwards with the blow, Danny grabbed the red inflation cords and tugged. Without a seconds delay he turned on the other guy as he flinched away from his partner flying backwards in an inflated lifejacket.

Danny grabbed the wrist of his gun hand and pushed it towards the front of the plane. Jarred by the sudden movement, the man's finger pulled on the trigger several times, sending bullets ripping through the curtain between the plane and cockpit, one of them punching a neat hole in the back of the pilot's head. The plane took a near vertical dive as the dead pilot slumped over the controls, sending Danny and the two men grappling with each other as they flew weightlessly into the cargo area. Tia shrieked as she remained locked in her seat by the seatbelt, her hair standing on end above her head.

The seconds felt like minutes until the co-pilot reached forward and heaved the controls back, levelling the plane and sending the three men crashing down on top of the boxes and crates in the back, their guns clattering away between the cargo.

'What's going on back there? Have you got him?' the co-pilot shouted in Spanish from the cockpit.

'Just hurry up and land at the estate. Delgado's guards can take care of him,' the man with the lifejacket and bloodied nose shouted back, yanking the lifejacket back off his head.

Danny was on the attack first, kicking out from his position on top of a crate to catch the other guy square in the jaw. Leaping to his feet, Danny dived at the guy with the bloodied nose while he reached between the crates to retrieve his gun. The man was quick. He came in with a combination of body blows and one to Danny's head, sending him thudding into the large cargo door on the left-hand side of the plane. Shaking it off, Danny grabbed the man's jacket by the collar and powered his knee into the guy's kidneys before whipping his elbow up to cracking it under the man's chin. His head whipped back and clanged on the door. Danny was about to go in for the kill when a shout from behind stopped him.

'Hey, *gringo*, back away.'

Danny turned to see a gun pointing at his head. He put his hands up and backed away.

'You ok, Pablo?'

'No, I think the fucker's broken my ribs.'

'Bastard. I say we throw him out of the cargo door,' the guy said, switching to Spanish so Danny wouldn't understand.

Pablo straightened up as best he could and grinned before pulling the lever to open the door. There was an ear popping rush of air and influx of engine noise as the door moved inside the plane on a rail top and bottom. Danny watched the man's eyes closely. The minute they flicked over to Pablo, he spun and planted a backward kick into Pablo's middle. The blow kicked him straight out the door where he seemed to hang in midair for a second, a look of terror locked on his face before the wind and the speed of the plane made him shoot off sideways, disappearing behind the aircraft.

Satisfied he'd taken at least one of them out, Danny turned to accept his fate. The deafening sound of gunshot filled the plane. To his surprise, he felt no pain. He looked up, confused to see the gunman looking at him in shock and surprise before dropping to the floor, a bullet hole in the centre of his back, with Tia standing behind him holding Pablo's gun.

'Hey, what's going on back there? Did you get him?' the co-pilot shouted from up front.

'He's asking if they got you,' Tia said, translating the co-pilot's Spanish.

'Er. *Si. Si*,' Danny yelled back, shrugging at Tia.

'Good, the estate is up ahead. Take a seat. I'm coming around to land.'

Danny looked at Tia.

'He's coming in to land at Delgado's estate,' she said.

Danny looked out of the cargo door to see Delgado's house and grounds pass under them as the plane went out over the cliffs to bank around over the Caribbean Sea on its approach to the airstrip.

'Tia, come with me and repeat what I say,' Danny said, picking up the other gun next to the body on the floor.

She followed him up into the cockpit and stood next to him while he shoved the barrel of his gun against the co-pilot's head.

'Do as I say. Fly low over the airstrip, but do not land.'

Danny paused while Tia translated.

'You can't shoot me. The plane will crash and we'll all be dead,' the co-pilot said defiantly.

'Tell him I have a pilot's licence and will blow his brains out and fly the goddamn plane myself if he doesn't do as I say,' Danny growled back angrily after Tia had translated the pilot's response.

As Tia translated, the co-pilot's face dropped. He nodded solemnly to indicate he would do as he was told.

Lowering his gun, he turned to Tia. 'Cover him, and for god's sake don't shoot him. I haven't got a clue how to fly this piece of crap,' he said, keeping his voice angry for the co-pilot's benefit. 'You fly, or bang bang. Ok?'

Leaving Tia pointing her gun at the co-pilot, Danny pulled the dead pilot out of the seat beside them and dragged his body out into the cargo area, placing him next to the man Tia shot by the open cargo door. Looking out at the airstrip just ahead of him, Danny could see one of the twins who'd kidnapped Scott from Brazil. He stood at the side of the airstrip in front of five armed men dressed in army-like fatigues. As the plane flew low over the airstrip, Danny threw Pablo out first, followed by the pilot. He could see the anger on the twins' faces as plain as day and as he looked up at the house, he could have sworn he saw Scott and Tia's husband Luis looking up at him from the pool terrace. A second later the estate was behind them. Danny shut the cargo door and headed back to the cockpit.

'Ok, we can't go to Santa Marta. I'm sure Delgado will have people waiting for us. Tia, the village your family is from, does it have any fields or roads? Somewhere we could land a plane?'

'*Si*, er, yes, it has fields.'

'Good, tell him where to go.'

TWENTY ONE

Scott and Luis were taking a short break after a morning of cracking code. The noise of an approaching aircraft piqued their curiosity, so they moved out onto the pool terrace for a look.

'What do you think? Is the man himself returning?' Scott said, watching the plane turning over the sea before heading back to land.

'No, he has his own plane, the one you arrived on. That one is cargo, probably supplies,' Luis replied, his hand up to block the sun's glare as he tried to get a better look.

'Mmm, he's still too high. He'll overshoot the landing strip. What is he doing? A fly past before he lands, perhaps?'

'I don't know. Look, the cargo door is open,' Luis said, seeing movement inside the plane.

Much to their surprise, a body came flying out of the opening. They watched it fall and bounce on the grassy airstrip before looking back up at the plane. A second body appeared in the opening, limp and lifeless with another man's arms hoisting it up from behind. They watched in amazement as it went the same way as the first, leaving a figure standing in the doorway in its place. He remained there for a few seconds, staring defiantly at Felipe and Delgado's men before sliding the cargo door shut. Scott smiled as he watched the plane continue low over the treetop before gaining height and turning to the west.

'Good morning, Daniel, nice of you to drop by,' Scott said with a smile as he raised his coffee cup in a salute.

'What, you know him?' Luis said in surprise.

'Yes I do, my good fellow, and I have a feeling you will too before long.'

Shouts from the airstrip drew their attention to the twin, Felipe. He was hopping mad, shouting at his men to clear the airstrip of the bodies.

'Come on, Luis, old man, I think with the current mood around here it might be a good idea to show some willing and get back to work,' Scott said, finishing his coffee.

'Yes, I think that would be a very good idea.'

The two of them walked back inside and headed for the computer room. They jumped back before they got there as the other twin, Rico, burst out of the room beside them. He threw them a sideways look that could kill, then rushed off towards the airstrip with a mobile phone held to his ear. They could still hear his raised voice talking at a hundred miles an hour to Delgado as they turned to continue on their way.

'He's telling him about your friend.'

'Yes, Daniel does tend to evoke that kind of reaction in people,' Scott replied, his curiosity causing him to gaze through the door Rico had left open. Inside was what must have been Balthasar Delgado's home office. 'What have we here then? Luis, old man, keep an eye out for a minute while I take a little peek,' Scott said, stepping inside.

'No Scott, come back. You will get us killed.' Luis said, looking around nervously.

Scott wasn't listening. He'd spotted the computer monitor on the office desk, still displaying the logged-on home screen from Delgado's computer.

'My, my, what a careless thing to do,' Scott muttered, smiling to himself as he rifled through the computer's program files and network settings.

'Scott, there is someone coming,' Luis said in a panicky voice through the open doorway.

'Just a couple more seconds.'

Luis turned to look back along the corridor. He could hear approaching footsteps coming in from the pool terrace. He looked back in at Scott tapping away on the keyboard, then back to the corridor.

'Oh, Jesus Christ, hurry up. Damn it,' he muttered before scooting along the corridor, bumping straight into Felipe as he turned the corner at the end.

'What are you doing? Get back to work,' Felipe growled angrily.

'Sorry, I just wondered what was going on over there on the airstrip,' Luis stammered out, trying to delay

Felipe.

'That's none of your concern. Now get back to work.'

'I say, you don't have to be so rude. We were just curious. It's not everyday you see people thrown out of a plane. I do hope they weren't friends of yours,' Scott said with more of a hint of sarcasm as he appeared behind Luis.

'Back to work. Now.'

'Come, Luis, my dear chap, let's leave him to calm down before he throws his teddies out of the pram,' Scott said, turning and walking away.

Felipe followed them back towards the computer room, pulling the door to Delgado's office shut the second he realised he'd left it open. Scott and Luis sat down in their chairs and scanned all the screens while running the code breaking programs created by Scott.

'What were you doing in Delgado's office?' Luis said as soon as Felipe got bored and left the room.

'There's another old saying in England, Luis, my dear fellow. People who live in glass houses shouldn't throw stones,' Scott said, changing the view on a screen.

He tapped away, the cursor and folders moving through security and network settings at lightning speed. In no time at all Balthasar Delgado's personal computer files filled the screen.

'What are you going to do with them?'

'I'm not sure yet, something suitably creative. Bingo,' Scott said, grinning as he flicked Delgado's hacked computer files off his screen to look at a new network appearing on one of the other monitors.

'Where is it?'

'Er, let me see, it's the CUMC campus network at Antonio Nariño University, in a place called Buenaventura.'

'Can we get in from there?'

'We should be able to. It's attached to the national schools network, which is all part of the government mainframe,' Scott said, zooming around the CUMC campus network at great speed.

'So what do we do now?'

'Well now, the game has changed. Instead of trying to break AES encryption, we are looking for back doors, links to move up the network towards the national electoral roll program. It'll take some time, but I should be able to do it.' Scott said with his usual air of superiority.

'It is true what they say about you. You are a genius, my friend,' Luis said, moving over to look at what Scott was doing.

'I know. It's a gift.' Scott said with a smile.

'Can we do it in time? The election is in three days.'

'Timing is everything, my dear fellow. Fingers crossed we won't have to. But if we do, I need to make sure we have a few aces up our sleeves.'

TWENTY TWO

'Thank you, Governor. Remember, vote Balthasar Delgado for President. We're going to build more schools, give bigger education budgets, invest in the youth of today for a better tomorrow,' Delgado said, shaking the school governor's hand while turning on a million-dollar smile for the gathering of press and news crews.

'Señor Delgado, what do you say to the allegations that your campaign is funded off the back of drugs money?'

'Thank you all for coming. That's all for today. Remember to vote for Balthasar Delgado for a brighter future for Colombia,' Delgado said speaking loudly, with total disregard for the man in the crowd.

Garcia moved beside him as he waved and headed for the car.

'That is the third time that cockroach of a journalist has turned up at one of my visits. Get him before he leaves,' Delgado whispered into Garcia's ear.

Garcia moved swiftly away without saying a word. He circled the crowd and headed for one of the cars in Delgado's cavalcade. The window lowered for him to speak to the men inside. As he walked away to re-join Delgado, his phone rang. Behind him, two of his men got out of the car and moved into the crowd. They stood on either side of the journalist, one whispering in his ear as the other pressed a gun into his side. The journalist's face went pale as they backed him out of the crowd and escorted him back to the car. After pushing him into the middle of the back seat, they got in either side to sandwich him as he trembled in the middle.

'I have a call from Rico,' Garcia said when he was back at Delgado's side.

'I'll take it in the car,' Delgado said quietly, leaving Garcia to go to the car ahead of him while he waved to the children, teachers, and the press before following.

The driver held the door open for him as he got in. Delgado waited until the door was shut and the car was moving before taking the phone off Garcia.

'Rico.'

'We have a problem, Señor Delgado. Pearson and Tia Rojas got on one of our planes at La Vanguardia Airport. Pablo and Jarell got on board to make sure there was no trouble when the pilot landed here at the estate.'

'Get to the point, Rico, what is the problem?' Delgado growled impatiently.

'When we went out to meet the plane it didn't land. It did a low pass while Pearson threw the bodies of Pablo and the pilot out. I don't know what happened to Jarell. The plane turned towards Santa Marta as it left.'

'Christ, will no one rid me of this infernal man. Have you been in touch with Jhon in Santa Marta?'

'Yes, the plane never reached the airport. It dropped below the radar around fifteen kilometres west of here.'

'Ok. Rico, take a dozen men and go out into the forest. Find them.'

'There are only a few hours of daylight left. We cannot track them in the dark. It would be better to set out at first light tomorrow,' Rico said, not sure if Delgado would explode, angry at the delay.

Delgado ground his teeth angrily, but knew Rico was right. 'Tell the soldiers at the coca fields and processing plants to look out for them. Leave at first light, I want them found and found quickly. Do you hear me, Rico?' Delgado yelled.

'Yes boss. Should I take Felipe with me?'

'No, leave your brother there. I want him to keep an eye on Miller and Rojas.'

'Ok.'

When Balthasar Delgado had hung up, the car fell into a nervous silence. The driver and Garcia knew better than to voice any opinions when their boss—with his well earned nickname, El Diablo—was so worked up.

'Take me to the warehouse on Calle 22.'

The three cars headed off, driving for about fifteen minutes before turning through some rusty, old, open gates. They crossed the car park and turned into an old abandoned warehouse, circling in the middle to form a horseshoe shape. Delgado got out of the lead car with Garcia. His two men in the middle car and the two in the rear one got out, pushing the journalist in front of them.

'You know who I am?' Delgado said, his face stern but voice calm.

The trembling man nodded weakly.

'Say it,' Delgado suddenly shouted at him.

'Balthasar Delgado.'

'No, say who I really am,' Delgado growled, inches from his face.

'El Diablo,' the reporter said, his voice cracking with fear.

'That's right, I am El Diablo, and you dare embarrass me in front of those people.'

'I'm sorry, I, I apologise, I will never speak of it again, I, I promise.'

'What is your name?'

'Emil, Emil Diaz, please let me go. You will never see me again,' Emil said, tears rolling down his trembling cheeks.

'Do you know how I got my nickname, El Diablo, Emil? No? I got it because I never let my enemies go. I track them and their families down then I kill the family in front of them, slowly. When, and only when, I see defeat in their eyes do I dispatch them to hell. Are you my enemy, Emil?'

'No, Señor, please, I will do whatever you want, just don't kill me,' Emil spouted as quickly as he could.

'Perhaps it is your lucky day, Emil. I am a busy man

and rather fond of this suit. I wouldn't want to get blood on it,' Delgado said, stepping back with a smile.

Emil took a deep breath, smiling out of a mixture of fear and relief.

'See you in hell, Emil,' Delgado said, his eyes flicking up as he nodded to his man behind Emil.

He felt no pain as the razor-sharp blade cut across his neck. Blood sprayed out as the arteries opened up, the sticky red fluid flowing down his severed windpipe, choking him. Emil put his hands to his throat in a desperate attempt to piece it back together. As he coughed up bubbles of blood and fell to the floor, Delgado lost interest and got back in the car. His men did the same, the horseshoe of cars driving around Emil's convulsing body, leaving him alone on the cold concrete to die in the empty warehouse.

'Take me back to the campaign headquarters, and find out if Arvin has found the woman yet,' Delgado said, his mind moving onto other things, Emil already forgotten.

'And if he has?'

'Tell him I want her back here. I want to look into this man Pearson's eyes while I kill her slowly.'

They drove on through the streets of Bogotá, pulling up at the campaign headquarters just as Garcia got hold of Arvin.

'Arvin has found her. She's staying in a small hotel in Montego Bay.'

'Good, tell him to charter a small plane, one with a pilot that will take the money and ask no questions.

Then get the girl and bring her to the estate.'

As soon as the message was relayed, Delgado flicked the switch, letting the politician's smile and false sincerity wash across his face. He got out of the car, shook a few people's hands, and entered his campaign offices.

'Good afternoon, everyone, how are we doing in the polls?'

'I'm afraid we are still down ten points on the opposition, Mr Delgado,' a nervous-looking university graduate intern said.

'Don't worry, my friend, we'll make up the difference by voting day,' Delgado said, smiling as he dismissed him to chat to the other campaign workers.

The visit lasted about an hour. Delgado played his candidate role perfectly, all smiles and motivational enthusiasm before waving and heading out the door to cheers and handclaps. The second he closed the car door his face turned to a frown and his eyes blazed furiously.

'Diego, call Felipe. I want him to make sure Miller and Rojas are making progress. We're ten points down on the polls and need that electoral roll program hacked for the ballot. I will not lose this election,' Delgado growled.

TWENTY THREE

With his gun relaxed but still in his hand on his lap, Danny spoke through Tia to make the pilot drop below radar height a few miles from the village where Tia grew up. They skimmed over the thick rainforest canopy below until it opened out over a village on the banks of a meandering river. There was a long strip of grassland running through the middle of the dozen or so houses, leading to rough, uneven fields containing crops.

'Ask him if he can land it there?'

Tia translated while Danny waited for the pilot's response to come back.

'He said, you're supposed to be a pilot, you tell him,' Tia said.

Danny's eyes narrowed and his face went taut. He leant in. 'Just land the damn plane,' he said through gritted teeth while pointing down with one hand and pushing his gun into the pilot's ribs with the other.

'Ok, ok,' the pilot replied quickly, no need for a translation from Tia.

Danny strapped himself into the pilot's seat beside the co-pilot while Tia went and buckled up in the cargo area. They passed very low over the village, scattering the people wandering into the proposed landing strip, curious at the noise of the engines. On the second run, the pilot dropped sharply over the river, flying between the tin-roofed buildings, the wing tips only inches from the block-walled sides. The wheels touched down hard on the grassland, bouncing a couple of times before the plane remained on the deck. The pilot pulled hard on the flaps, stamping on the brakes as he tried to slow the plane before it overshot the village into a field full of a crop of tall corn. He failed. The plane hit the soft dirt, bouncing up and down as corn plants flew high into the air, shredded by the propellers until the plane finally came to a halt.

'Are you ok?' Danny said, sliding out of the seat belt to look back at Tia.

'Yes, I'm fine.'

He started to move toward the back of the plane then stopped and turned to look at the plane's instrument panel. Lifting a leg he stomped down hard on the radio unit, directing all his weight through his heel into the little LCD screen and multitude of buttons. The co-pilot jumped as the screen starred and blinked before dying as half the buttons disappeared inside the metal casing, followed by a puff of smoke. Ignoring him, Danny moved into the back and pulled open the cargo door. Three angry villagers stood in the shredded corn, pointing M-16 rifles at him.

'Whoa, fellas, take it easy. You speak English?'

'Who are you? You work for Delgado?' A large middle-aged man in the middle said.

'Put the gun down, Uncle. This is Danny. He's a friend.'

'Tia, is that you?' he replied, lowering the gun before shielding his eyes from the sun to see inside the plane's dark interior.

There was a rapid exchange of Spanish as she hopped down from the plane and hugged each of the three guys in turn.

'Sorry. Danny, this is my uncle, Edgar Alvarez, my cousin Miguel, and my brother Samuel.'

Danny hopped down and gave them a nod.

'Tia tells me her husband Luis and your friend are being held by Delgado at his estate,' Edgar said.

'That's right, I'm going to get them back,' Danny said without hesitation.

'On your own?' said Tia's brother Samuel.

'If I have to,' Danny replied, his face deadly serious.

'You're *loco*, man. You won't even find the place, let alone get inside,' Samuel said, shaking his head.

'Then help me, show me where it is.'

'Who's that?' Edgar said, jumping at movement inside the plane.

'Co-pilot, one of Delgado's,' Danny said, looking round to see the man lurking around in the cargo hold.

The three men instantly raised their rifles. The co-pilot panicked, raising his hands while talking quickly. There was a lot of conversation and pointing, then silence as the co-pilot jumped down from the plane. He turned and ran through the chopped-up corn, turning onto the dirt track that led out of the village before disappearing into the forest.

'What did he say?' Danny said, surprised they let him go.

'He said he had no choice and I believe him. Delgado's right-hand man, Diego Garcia, told him and the pilot to fly you and his two men to his estate, no questions asked. He said that people who let El Diablo down are never seen again,' said Tia's Uncle Edgar.

'What did you say?'

'I said follow the dirt track for five kilometres. It joins the main road to Santa Marta. He can hitch a ride from there.'

'Will you help me get to Delgado's estate?' Danny asked, looking Edgar in the eye.

'Balthasar Delgado has driven us off our land and killed people we love. For my niece and her husband, for you and for everyone in the village, I will help you.'

'I will help you too,' said Samuel.

'So will I,' said Miguel.

'Thank you,' Danny smiled, while Tia moved in and hugged her uncle.

'But we will have to wait until tomorrow. It will be dark soon, and it's many miles through the rainforest to the estate. Come, you are my guest. You dine with us tonight,' said Edgar, leading them out of the field towards the village.

Edgar's house was the largest in the village, built of

concrete blocks, rendered and painted white. Wooden steps led up to a veranda built all around the house, its ground floor over six feet off the ground in case the river flooded badly in the rainy season. The inside was surprisingly spacious, neat and tidy, with Edgar's house-proud wife, Maria, moving around them offering food and drinks.

Through the course of the evening Danny learned how the Alvarez family used to live and farm next to Balthasar Delgado's father and grandfather. When Balthasar came of age and took over the farm, he soon tired of the hard work and small profits. He preferred to grow Marijuana plants and then moved onto coca plants for cocaine, America's growing appetite for the drug eating up all he could supply. Soon the Delgado estate grew and more and more men arrived, armed men, mercenaries. They used intimidation and violence to drive the Alvarez family off their land. When they fought back, they killed Tia's father and mother. When the rest of the family reported it to the authorities, they found Delgado had them in his pocket and the case was dropped. Danny could see this was still raw for Edgar, who had to go outside for a breath of fresh air while Tia's brother, Samuel Alvarez, told the story. The evening eventually wound down and Edgar showed Danny to his room for the night.

'Thank you for getting my niece away from that monster. We'll leave just after sun up, my friend. Get a good night's sleep,' Edgar said, patting Danny on the back.

'You're welcome. You sure you and the others want to come with me?' Danny said, turning to face him.

'We are sure, my friend. It is long overdue.'

Danny smiled, shook his hand and went to bed.

TWENTY FOUR

Nikki sat on a sun lounger by the pool of a small boutique hotel she'd found in Montego Bay. The view of the beach and Caribbean Sea across the road from the hotel should have been a tourist's dream. But Nikki was only there because the alternative of sitting in her room waiting for news from Danny was worse than sitting around the pool. She'd called several times but his phone had gone straight to answer phone, which only set her mind spinning further.

Nikki managed around an hour before doing nothing drove her crazy. She took a walk down the road to take her mind off things, down towards the colourfully named Doctor's Cave Beach and the tourist area of Montego Bay. She politely fended off the advances of the street sellers trying to catch tourists with shell necklaces and bracelets. Walking away from them, Nikki noticed a man walking around twenty metres behind her, his classic Hispanic features instantly putting her on edge. He talked on his phone as he walked, his eyes looked in her direction, but in an uninterested, looking through her rather than at her way. The way you would if your mind is on something else. She shook the feeling off, but turned into a market full of little craft and souvenir shops, just in case. Glancing back, she was thankful to see the man continue along the beach road. Relaxing a little, Nikki looked around the shops and stalls. She bought herself a little souvenir beaded necklace, then headed back towards the beach through a narrow alley between the shops. Just before she reached the end of the alley, the Hispanic man swung into view, staring straight at her, this time with intent. His approach was quick, meaningful and intimidating. Acting on Danny's words of wisdom, act now and ask questions later, Nikki swung her bag in his face as hard as she could before turning on her heels and running back to the shops, shouting, 'Help me, there's a man chasing me!'

A few locals stepped forward to help, backing away wide-eyed at the sight of Arvin pulling a gun out from under his light jacket. Coming back to the main walkway, Nikki looked towards the beach, turning away and heading towards the rear of the complex when she saw it was blocked full of tourists. She kicked off her flip-flops and ran full pelt for what looked like a car park beyond the walkway between the shops. A glance behind her confirmed she was opening the gap between herself and the guy with the gun. Running between the shops, she made a beeline for a park in the distance.

A figure appeared in front of her from behind the last

shop, his arm raised as he cracked the butt of his handgun in between her eyes. The force of the blow added with the momentum of her running knocked her clean off her feet, leaving her lying flat on her back, dazed and confused. She was vaguely aware of Roberto and Arvin picking her up and bundling her in the back of a rusty van. It set off noisily, bouncing her around in the back as the knackered rear shocks failed to handle the bumps in the road.

The tears and fuzzy vision started to clear after a few minutes. Nikki tried to sit up, but the sharp pain in her head kept her lying on the floor of the van for another few minutes. When she eventually managed to spin around on the floor and look up over the driver and passenger seats, Arvin looked back at her, his gun pointed at her head as he twisted in his seat.

'Just sit right back down, lady,' Arvin said in broken English.

They drove for twenty minutes or so, following the coast road, eventually stopping well away from any built-up areas somewhere to the west of the city. The side door slid open and the harsh sunlight sent stabbing pains through Nikki's head, like she'd been hit for a second time. Arvin and Roberto dragged her out. She could feel sand under her feet as they guided her, one on either side. As the pain subsided, Nikki opened her eyes to see a small seaplane with its skids right up against the beach. Splashing through the gentle waves, Arvin and Roberto manhandled her onto one of the skids, then pushed her inside. By the time they'd shoved her into the seat at the back, the door had shut and the pilot was starting the engine.

'You're sure you have enough fuel to get us there?' Arvin shouted to the pilot over the engine noise.

'Ya man, we good. All I need is the other half of the money, and the fuel for the return journey,' the pilot said. His dreadlocks swung as he turned around to give them a wide grin, showing a mass of white teeth and a couple of gold ones.

'You'll get your money when we get there, and we have aviation fuel at the estate. How long will the journey take?'

'About four hours, man, no problem,' the pilot said, turning back and throttling up the aircraft, bouncing and skipping it across the sea until it took off.

Roberto and Arvin looked at each other a little nervously, the strong smell of marijuana coming from the front not giving them much confidence.

'So who's the pretty young girl then?' the pilot asked once they were airborne.

'None of your fucking business,' Arvin shouted back.

'Ok, ok, be cool, I'm just trying to make conversation.'

'Just fly the plane,' Arvin said, disgruntled.

'Whatever you say, man, it's your dollar, you da boss.'

TWENTY FIVE

'Why are you not working?' Felipe said to Scott and Luis, his manner decidedly more aggressive than usual.

'My, my, did one get out the wrong side of the bed this morning?' Scott replied, deliberately picking his coffee cup up slowly to take a sip from it.

Felipe stepped in fast, swiping Scott's coffee cup from his hands, sending it flying onto the pool terrace where it shattered into pieces, making Luis jump out of his skin.

'Señor Delgado wants to know how close you are to completing the program,' he said, placing his knuckles on the table as he leant in to intimidate Scott.

'Well, perhaps Señor Delgado would like to get off his backside and come and ask me himself,' Scott said defiantly.

Scott barely got the last word out before Felipe pulled a gun from his shoulder holster and shoved it in his face. It trembled slightly as Felipe fought to control his temper, and the temptation to blow Scott's brains out.

'Careful, old man, anything happens to me and I'm

guessing I won't be the only one looking at the wrong end of a gun,' Scott said perfectly calmly.

Scott held Felipe's angry stare for what felt like an eternity.

'Get back to work,' Felipe said, finally backing down to break the stalemate.

Scott got out of his chair slowly and followed Luis inside.

'You push him too far,' Luis said when they got back to the computer room.

'One has to take one's victories where one can, dear boy,' Scott said, watching another *Access Granted* screen pop up on the monitor.

'Which one is that?'

'Bogotá City Council. Almost there, Luis, old chap, just got the government firewall to crack and we are in.'

'How long do you think?'

'A few hours for the firewall, and the rest of the day to re-code the electoral program. We should be all finished sometime this evening. The election is on Friday, right?'

'Yes, the day after tomorrow, we are safe until then,' Luis said, his eyes dropping to the floor.

'You're worried about your wife, aren't you?'

'Yes, I haven't spoken to her for three days. I worry Delgado has killed her,' Luis said, on the verge of tears.

'Have faith, Luis, I'm sure she will be ok, until after the election anyway,' said Scott, stopping his typing to put his hand on Luis's shoulder.

'But what then?'

'I'm hoping things will get a little more exciting

around here before then,' Scott said with a smile.

'Your friend, Mr Pearson. But what can he do against Delgado and all his men?'

'You might be pleasantly surprised, dear boy. Daniel is not someone you want to wage a war against.'

Luis looked at Scott unconvinced, before both men got back to hacking the firewall to the government's internal computer network.

TWENTY SIX

The flight from Jamaica had been long and tiresome. Nikki sat at the back, her head throbbing from Roberto's strike and the loud engine noise. The pilot banked the plane when Santa Marta came into view, putting his shades on against the glare of the sinking sun. He flew parallel to the remote rainforest-topped cliffs, the turquoise Caribbean Sea crashing on the rocks below them. Around twenty minutes later, Arvin pointed out a small jetty with a speedboat moored on one side. A line of steps carved out of the cliff led up to the airstrip and the Delgado estate.

'Hey man, where am I going to refuel?' the pilot said, easing the plane down for landing.

'I'll get the men to bring barrels down from the airstrip,' said Arvin.

'And my money?' the pilot said, the setting sun glinting off his gold teeth as he grinned at Arvin.

'He has your money,' Arvin said, pointing down at Felipe standing on the jetty with two armed men behind him.

'Ok man, down we go then.'

He landed the plane smoothly onto the calm sea, cutting the engine just short of the jetty to drift the rest of the way and float gently up beside it. Jumping out first, the pilot tied a rope off at the front and back to moor the plane tightly to the wooden walkway, then stood back out of the others' way. Arvin got out first while Roberto grabbed Nikki roughly by the arm, manhandling her out of the plane where Arvin took her arm and led her away.

'Ok, boss man, you got my money, yeah?' the pilot said, walking up to Felipe.

'You told no one about this trip?'

'Nah man, no one, just like your man there told me.'

Climbing the steps up the cliff with Arvin breathing down her neck, Nikki looked back just in time to see Felipe pull his gun and shoot the pilot in the head. His body stayed upright for a few seconds, taking its time to realise the commands from the brain had ceased before flopping to the ground.

'You two, take his body out in the boat and feed it to the sharks. Refuel and clean the plane when you get back. Jhon can take it back with him to Santa Marta when he's here next week,' said Felipe turning to glare at Nikki.

Horrified, she turned away and carried on up the steps on her bare feet to the airstrip. They escorted her through the gate and into the estate. Felipe took over from Arvin and Roberto, grabbing her roughly by the wrist to lead her inside, his gun still gripped tightly in his other hand.

'Where's my brother?' she protested, pulling back.

'You want to see your brother, fine. Let's go and see your brother,' Felipe said, a smile forming on his face.

Felipe pulled her through the house and down the corridor to the computer room. He shouted for the guard outside to open the door before storming in with Nikki. Scott and Luis jumped in their seats at the sudden intrusion, the surprise turning to concern when Scott realised Nikki was standing beside Felipe.

'Nikki, are you alright? They haven't hurt you, have they?' Scott said, getting out of his seat at the sight of the bruise between Nikki's eyes.

'Sit back down. You only have one day left to get access to the voting system. If not, you can say goodbye to your sister,' Felipe said, bringing his gun up to place the barrel on the side of her head.

Scott sat down slowly, his eyes never leaving Felipe's. 'It's done. I have direct access to the government server and have already altered the voting reports system. Now let me start again. Are you alright, Nikki? This oaf hasn't hurt you at all?'

'I'm ok, it looks worse than it is,' Nikki replied, pleased to see her brother alive.

'Then we only need you to run the program on Friday during the election,' Felipe said, his gun moving from Nikki's head to Luis's.

Scott turned to the computer and started hitting keys rapidly. Within seconds, all six screens blinked to a lockout screen with two passcode boxes, a number below each box.

'Do you know what this is? No, of course you don't, you caveman. This is a dual algorithm passcode entry system. I built it because I thought you'd do something like this. In simple terms, just for you, I apply a formula, which only I know, to the number below the box. The answer is my passcode to enter the system. My dear Luis here has his own formula, known only to him. If we don't both enter the correct codes at the same time, this computer will alert the government server to an illegal access and shut the whole thing down. Your choice, dear boy: kill Luis and you won't get in, hurt my sister and I'll enter the wrong code and fry the lot. Good luck with explaining that to Mr Delgado.'

The tension in the room was stifling. Felipe moved his gun from Luis to Scott to Nikki. His eyes burned furiously at being outsmarted by Scott.

'Take her away,' he eventually said to the guard on the door, waiting until she was out of the room before he left, slamming the door behind him.

'Thank you, my friend. You have saved my life again. What was all that about formulas?'

'Well, I couldn't jolly well tell him you just enter the number below the box now, could I?' Scott said with a grin.

'It was very quick thinking, but I fear it has only bought us a little more time.'

'Yes, until Friday night. I hope that's long enough. The formula charade has given me an idea though. To work, my dear Luis, to work.'

TWENTY SEVEN

Edgar woke Danny up just after sun-up. He sat up and rubbed his eyes, spotting a pile of neatly pressed and folded green fatigues on the chair in the corner when they focused. A pair of combat boots sat under the chair and a hunting knife in a leather sheath lay on top of the clothes. He dressed and made his way outside. Maria handed him some scrambled eggs and tomatoes wrapped up in hot bread on his way out. Miguel and Samuel stood next to Edgar by an old, battered pickup truck, while Tia sat in the passenger seat of the truck, her arm resting on the open window frame.

'No, sorry, Tia, get out of the truck. You can't come. It's too dangerous,' Danny said, walking over.

Tia looked out of the truck, her face unlike Danny had seen the day before. It looked hard, determined, and angry.

'Hold on there, man, you obviously don't know Tia that well. She can track her way through the rainforest better than any of us, and she's the best shot in the village,' her brother Samuel said with a grin.

'Yeah, don't go upsetting her. She'll put you on your arse,' Miguel chipped in.

Danny looked at both of them and then at Tia stepping out of the truck. She looked totally different in her green fatigues and army boots. After a steely-eyed stare at Danny, she grabbed an M-16 rifle, tucked the butt into her shoulder and looked down the sights like she'd done it a thousand times before. Drawing a deep breath, she exhaled half before holding it as she squeezed the trigger gently. Six hundred metres away, a hubcap hanging from a large tree near the river clanged and swung around violently on its rope.

Danny turned back towards the truck and walked past Tia. 'Ok, ready whenever you are.'

Edgar climbed into the driver's seat while Danny, Miguel and Samuel climbed into the back with the backpacks and M-16 rifles.

'What's in the bags?' Danny said.

'Food, ammunition, two-way radios, oh, and a little dynamite,' Miguel said with a grin.

'Dynamite?'

'Yeah, we do a little blasting up in the mountains.'

'Blasting for what?'

'Emeralds mostly, the odd ruby or small diamond, not riches, but enough to support the village and send our kids to school,' said Miguel.

'Don't you have to worry about a mining company moving in?'

'Nah, this entire area is protected. It's all national park

as far as the eye can see.'

'Don't you worry about getting caught?' said Danny.

'Look around you, bro, ain't no one here but us and a load of Delgado's coca farmers,' Miguel said with a big grin.

'I suppose not. That's the reason for the M-16's, Delgado's men?' Danny said, stripping and checking the weapon.

The truck rumbled slowly out of the village, along a bumpy dirt track, heading into the trees and dense undergrowth.

'Yeah, we liberated them from El Diablo's guards at one of his processing plants,' Samuel said.

'Where are the processing plants, at the estate?'

'Nah, Delgado keeps the estate clean. They process the cocaine in camps in the rainforest. It's remote and far away from prying eyes.'

'So how does Delgado move the cocaine?' Danny said.

'We don't know. He used to fly it out from the airfield. Plane after plane, they'd come and go all day and night. Then overnight, they stopped coming. Delgado paid his way into politics and gave out the squeaky clean image,' Samuel said, shrugging his shoulders.

'But where does all the cocaine go?'

'I don't know. We've seen them load the trucks at the processing plant. They head in the estate's direction, but Delgado has too many guards and mercenaries for us to follow,' Samuel said apprehensively.

Morning moved into afternoon, and the temperature

rose into the humid thirties. For hours the truck crawled along the muddy track. Edgar eventually turned off, crunching and snapping twigs as he flattened his way into the undergrowth. When the truck was far enough away from the track to be hidden, Edgar pulled it to a stop. Everyone jumped out of the back and started putting bags on their backs, checking weapons and kit.

'It's too dangerous to drive any further. We go on foot from here,' Edgar said to Danny.

'How far is the estate from here?' Danny asked, swinging his backpack on before grabbing an M-16 and following the others.

'It's about twelve kilometres in that direction, with the rainforest and avoiding Delgado's men. That's about twelve hours. We'll have to camp when it gets dark and should get to the estate around midday tomorrow.'

Danny just nodded and fell into line. He noticed Tia taking the lead, moving nimbly through the undergrowth like it was second nature to her. They kept moving, albeit slowly, through the dense undergrowth for a couple of hours. Even for Danny, with his former jungle training, it was hard to keep track of which direction they were going. He had to hand it to Tia. She was far tougher than he'd first given her credit for. She moved ever onward with no sign of slowing as she hacked a way forward with a machete. After trekking for another fifteen minutes, Tia's hand shot back with her palm up. Edgar, Miguel and Samuel lowered on their haunches and split out either side of Tia, melting into the vegetation as they lay on their fronts. Danny did the same, crawling forward to lie next to Tia.

'What is it?' he whispered.

'One of Delgado's processing plants up ahead.'

'Where? I don't see anything.'

'Smell?' she whispered back.

Danny breathed deeply through his nose and picked up the faint scent of petrol.

'Petrol?' Danny said, puzzled.

'Yes, petrol, er, gasoline. They soak the coca leaves in gasoline to separate the alkaloids before they dry them. When the leaves are dry, they go through several processes with a lime solution, acid, potassium and acetone. Eventually, they end up with a paste that dries into pure cocaine.'

'Where is it?'

Tia put her hand up, twisting it to feel the direction of the cool breeze in the sweat on her palm. 'Up there over that ridge, we should go around them,' she said, pointing in the opposite direction.

'How many people will Delgado have there?' Danny said, his stare and thoughts still directed at the ridge.

'He keeps them small, seven, eight workers maybe, and four or five armed guards. Why?'

'Feel like sending Delgado a message,' Danny said with a grin.

'Won't that just alert them we're coming?'

'After the plane yesterday, they already know we're coming. If we create some chaos out here, it'll draw more men out of the estate. And if we're going to get Scott and your husband out, the fewer people we've got to deal with at the estate, the better.'

Tia and Edgar looked at each other before nodding and turning back to him.

'Ok, what do you want us to do?'

TWENTY EIGHT

Danny, Tia and Miguel made their way cautiously to the top of the ridge. Edgar and Samuel circled around to the right and waited for Danny's command over the two-way radio. When they reached the top, they could hear a generator chugging away somewhere below them. The ground ahead dropped away to form a bowl-shaped dip. Several large green canvases were strung out tightly between the trees to form covers over the various stages of cocaine processing. They'd stacked a large quantity of metal gasoline drums on the far side of the camp. Row upon row of plastic containers sat next to the drums, full of chemicals to process the coca leaves into cocaine. Workers moved around under the covers, dressed in rags and sub-standard protective clothing, wearing tatty, ripped rubber boots and dirty plastic aprons with rubber gloves on their hands.

In the tent closest to them, the workers busied themselves soaking the coca leaves laid out on massive plastic sheets in gasoline. The other tents continued the process by either soaking the leaves in chemicals or drying them for the next stage. In the final tent they dried the white paste into finished pure cocaine, weighed it into kilo bricks and wrapped in cellophane.

Two armed men stood outside leaning on a waist-high stack of cocaine bricks as they talked. Danny counted another three armed men dotted around the camp. All of them looked bored with the mundane daily grind, the knowledge that they worked for Balthasar Delgado making an attack a ridiculous prospect, nobody would ever mess with El Diablo. Danny had other ideas.

'You in position?' Danny said quietly over the radio.

'Yeah, we're looking down on two guards by a stack of cocaine bricks,' Edgar replied.

'Ok, creep down and take them by surprise. We'll move down and take the three guards on this side. Only fire if you absolutely have to,' Danny said, hoping no one got trigger-happy.

The last thing he wanted was semi-automatic weapons spraying bullets across the camp. Most of the workers were probably exploited locals or farm hands, paid a pittance for breathing in chemicals all day to make Delgado even richer.

Danny moved down the slope with Tia and Miguel closely behind. They crouched down behind the large generator chugging away at the bottom of the dip, the smell of gasoline and chemicals burning their noses and making their eyes water a little. Looking out from behind the generator, Danny saw Edgar and Samuel moving swiftly down the slope on the far side, the two guards still facing away from them and still leaning on the stack of cocaine bricks. One of the other guards walked past them on the far side of the generator, stopping by a bush to take a pee.

'You take him, Tia. Miguel, follow me,' Danny whispered.

While Tia moved up behind the pissing guard, Danny and Miguel popped out from behind the generator, their M-16's raised at the two guards in the middle of the camp. Simultaneously, Tia shoved the barrel of her gun into the back of the pissing guard's neck, while Edgar and Samuel told the two by the cocaine stack to drop their weapons. Miguel shouted in Spanish for the two guards in the middle to drop their rifles. All the shocked guards did as they were told, while the workers froze where they were, looking out from under the canvas covers with frightened eyes.

They collected all the weapons, then moved everyone into the clearing in the middle of the camp.

'Edgar, tell them to go, get as far away from here as possible. Tell them a war is coming, it's coming for El Diablo.'

While Edgar translated, Danny, Miguel and Samuel started rolling gasoline drums into the covered areas. They undid the lids and let the gasoline glug out over the processing coca leaves, coughing as the fumes of the evaporating fuel stung their noses.

'Come on, let's make this quick. Just two more on the cocaine bricks and we can light the place up and get out of here,' Danny said, unscrewing all the caps on the gasoline barrels while keeping one eye on the last worker as he disappeared into the rainforest.

A few minutes later, they stood back up on the ridge above the camp. Miguel lit a rag hanging out of a bottle full of petrol and hurled it down on the river of gasoline running through the dirt all around the camp. The bottle broke, instantly disappearing from sight inside a huge ball of flame. The trails of gasoline ignited, shooting out towards the canvas-covered areas like lightning bolts. Huge balls of flame engulfed the coca leaves and cocaine stacks, burning through the canvas covers in seconds, sending great clouds of thick black smoke up through the tree canopy.

'If that doesn't bring them all out looking for us, I don't know what will,' Danny said, the heat from the fire making them move back.

'Yes, we need to go now, get away from here and find a safe place to camp for the night. It will be dark in a couple of hours,' Edgar said, turning away to head back into the rainforest.

They all turned and followed him, the tension killing all the jokes and chatter as they scanned the dense undergrowth for signs of movement. They'd only gone a few minutes into their journey when the remaining gasoline drums exploded back in the camp. The noise was deafening, setting off a chain reaction of shrieks and howls overhead from panicked birds and frightened monkeys in the trees. A huge, rising mushroom cloud of smoke plumed in the sky high above the tree canopy. Their bodies tensed knowing it was just a matter of when, not if, they were going to have to fight Delgado's men.

TWENTY NINE

Four kilometres away at the coca fields to the north of them, Rico stopped questioning a farm worker about the direction the plane went the day before. He turned with his men towards the sound of the explosion. A cloud of thick black smoke rose above the forest canopy in the distance.

'Quick, all of you, back to the truck,' he shouted, running out of the coca field.

Rico climbed into the passenger side of the cab, slamming the door shut. 'Go, go, go, turn it around.'

'There's no room,' the driver shrugged, looking at the narrow dirt track in front of him.

'Just turn it around. Now,' Rico growled, pulling his handgun out to hold it intimidatingly in his lap.

The driver immediately did as he was ordered. He bumped the truck off the dirt track and ploughed a circle through the coca crop, bouncing back up on the track to head off towards the rising smoke. The last of Delgado's soldiers running towards the back of the truck only just managing to get pulled in by the others as the it accelerated into the forest.

Fifteen minutes' drive down the track, they came across two of the guards from the camp running towards them, waving. The truck pulled to a halt and Rico wound the windows down.

'What happened?'

'Men with rifles attacked the camp, Señor Torres,' the guard said nervously.

'What men, what did they look like?' Rico said, looking down at them.

'A gringo, four Colombian men and a woman.'

'And you did nothing to stop them,' Rico said angrily.

'They came in so quickly, there was nothing we could do,' the guard said, not daring to look Rico in the face, the man next to him doing the same. 'They gave us a message to give to Señor Delgado.'

'Tell me,' Rico said, raising his voice.

'They said a war is coming. A war is coming for El Diablo,' the man said, his voice shaky as he spoke.

Rico stared at the man, his eyes burning furiously, his face tight as he ground his teeth angrily.

'Get in the back,' he eventually growled, barely waiting until they'd got in before he ordered the driver onward.

Pushed by Rico, the driver sped the truck along faster than he should for another ten minutes, the men in the back hanging on tightly to stop them flying about. They saw the smoke and smelled the mixture of burning fuel and chemicals before what was left of the camp came into sight. Rico and the driver got out of the vehicle. They stood looking at the smouldering remains while the two men from camp and Delgado's soldiers climbed out of the truck and stood behind them. Without warning, Rico turned, pulled his handgun out and locked his arm as he moved its aim between the two men from the camp.

'And you did nothing to stop this?'

Without a word, the soldiers backed away from the two men like they were cursed.

'But Señor Torres, there was nothing we could—'

Birds and animals cried out, startled by the sudden sound of gunfire. One man dropped to the floor before he got the last word out. Rico's gun immediately centred on the other man's head. He put his hands up in front of him and pleaded for his life. A second shot rang out, dropping the guard next to his unfortunate colleague.

'Spread out, you find anyone from the camp. Shoot them as a warning. Nobody fails El Diablo,' Rico shouted, tucking his gun back into its holster.

'What about the gringo and the others who did this?' the driver said to him.

'They will be far away by now and it will be dark soon. We'll camp here and hunt them down in the morning,' Rico said, the sound of a plane making him look up through the tree canopy.

Delgado's private plane flew overhead, circling around the rising smoke before turning to head in the estate's direction.

'Fetch me the radio,' Rico said.

Leave Nothing To Chance

THIRTY

Delgado's nine seater, twin turboprop Piaggio P-180 light aircraft turned over the Caribbean Sea. It descended to land gently on the airstrip next to the estate. Delgado and Garcia stepped out, squinting against the low sun to see Felipe heading their way, holding a radio in front of him.

'Rico,' Felipe said, handing it over.

Delgado marched away from the plane's winding-down propellers. He headed through the gate into the estate before taking the radio off Felipe and answering it.

'Rico.'

'Pearson and the woman took out the north processing plant. They had help.'

'Gringos?'

'No, Colombians, three of them, all armed with M-16's.'

Delgado turned to look out over the rainforest, deep in thought.

'It's getting dark. What do you need?'

'We will camp here tonight and start tracking them in the morning. Send the rest of the men in from the south first thing, we will trap them in the middle.'

'Ok good, and Rico?'

'Yes.'

'Find them and kill them. I have to return to Bogotá tonight. It's election day tomorrow. I can't afford to have any problems. Do you hear me, Rico?' Delgado said, turning back to the estate.

'Si señor, kill them.'

Joining the others, Delgado headed across the pool terrace to the house.

'Felipe, our troublesome friend has destroyed the north processing plant. Rico is there now. At first light, take all but a handful of men and drop them on the track near our south camp. Tell them to work their way towards Rico. He wants to trap them in the middle. I want them all dead. I will pay a big bonus to the one who kills this man, Pearson, OK?'

'Si señor.'

'Good, now find Quinto. Tell him to prepare some food for Diego and myself while I check on Miller's progress. We have to fly back to Bogotá in a couple of hours.'

While Felipe headed off, Delgado and Garcia walked past the grand staircase and headed for the computer room. Delgado waved aside the guard standing outside the door then entered the room.

'Ah, I wondered when our generous host would turn up,' said Scott sarcastically, without turning away from the keyboard.

'You have a smart mouth, Mr Miller. That may not work out so well for your sister,' Delgado said, his voice under control but the anger clearly detectable in its tone.

'Steady on, old boy, you wouldn't want me to terminate our little project before tomorrow's election now, would you?' Scott said, furiously tapping on the keyboards until a big *delete* box appeared in the centre of all six screens. Scott turned to look Delgado in the eye, his finger hovering over the return key.

There was an uneasy stalemate while both men held each other's gaze, Scott's finger never leaving the keyboard, daring Delgado to make him push it.

As if flicked by a switch, Delgado's face softened into a smile. 'Very good, Mr Miller. I apologise for my outburst. It's been a long day. Please, I hear you have obtained full access to the electoral results program. Show me.'

Scott waited a few seconds longer to assert his control over the situation, then slowly moved his finger to the escape key and pressed it. All the screens blinked back to normal. Just to show Delgado who had the power, if only in here in the computer room. Scott brought up the government's electoral results program with its rows of districts, parties, and votes.

'How does it work?' Delgado said, leaning in to look at all the information.

'I've created a program within the program. As the figures come in, it increases your results to show above the winning result. It does this randomly between four and seven percent, so nothing looks untoward. It's quite ingenious if I say so myself. You will need me to remove it once the election is over. If it were to be discovered later, officials would know someone tampered with the election. And unless you can pay off the entire government, you'd be kicked out of office and a re-election would be called for.'

'You are truly worthy of your reputation, Mr Miller. Excellent work. After tomorrow I will be President, and you will be on your way to Rio de Janeiro with your sister, two million dollars richer. Mr Rojas will be reunited with his wife and we will all be happy, no?' Delgado said, a politician's insincere smile fixed on his face.

'Mmm, if you say so.'

'Of course, I am a man of my word, Mr Miller,' Delgado said, patting Scott on the back before leaving the room.

Delgado and Garcia headed to the dining room, where the staff had set the table. Quinto brought a selection of cold meats, bread and salad in for them to eat.

'The last count will be in around midnight. By breakfast I will be President, my friend, and you will be Vice President,' Delgado laughed before raising a glass of wine to Garcia.

Garcia raised his glass in return, a concerned look still on his face.

'What is the matter, Diego? Are you not happy?'

'Of course, but I will be happier once these loose ends

are taken care of,' Garcia said, the concerned look still on his face.

Delgado took a sip of wine before putting the glass down.

'Do not worry, my friend, Felipe and Rico will find and take care of Pearson and the others in the morning. Once Mr Miller and Mr Rojas remove their program from the system, we will kill them too.' Delgado paused and took another sip of his drink before continuing. 'I think I will take the sister back with us tonight. I wish to celebrate after I win the election, before I kill her as well.'

THIRTY ONE

A hand shaking his shoulder awoke Danny with a start. He had his handgun up in the face of the blurred figure before his eyes had time to focus. When they did, Tia stood in front of him, a finger to her lips. The others stood behind her, looking more like a military unit than a family of farmers fighting to be free of a tyrant.

'Delgado's men are to the north, coming from the direction of the processing plant we hit yesterday. We must go now,' she whispered.

Danny jumped to his feet and kitted up, then followed Tia's lead into the dense forest.

'How far is the estate?' Danny asked after half an hour of trekking.

'It's about five kilometres. You will be able to see it once we get to the top of this hill,' Tia said, pointing up a steep incline.

They moved off at a fast pace up the hill. Danny followed, sweating and breathing heavily, unused to the humid heat of the rainforest as he kept pace with the others.

I'm definitely getting too old for this shit.

The ground eventually levelled off to a place where the trees parted to give them a spectacular view over the top of the rainforest. A flock of macaw parrots flew across their line of sight as they looked down the valley, their vivid red, yellow, and blue plumage standing out spectacularly against the rich green of the forest canopy. Delgado's estate was visible in the distance, sitting on the clifftop above the aquamarine Caribbean Sea. Danny shielded his eyes from the sun as he looked intently at the estate. It was too far away to get any great detail, but he could still make out a group of figures moving around next to a couple of trucks on the empty airstrip. He watched them get into the trucks before they moved onto the dirt road and disappeared out of sight into the forest.

'It looks like your plan to draw them out by torching the camp worked,' Edgar said from beside him.

'The only problem is they are coming straight for us,' said Miguel from the other side.

'I guess we'd better be careful then,' Tia said, walking past them down the other side of the slope towards the estate.

'I told you, you don't want to upset my sister,' said Samuel with a grin as he followed Tia.

Danny turned and looked back across the top of the rainforest canopy they'd just come through. A flock of startled birds cried out and took flight around half a kilometre away.

'They are not far behind us,' Danny said.
'Best we keep moving,' Edgar replied.
'Into Delgado's trap.'
'It's a big jungle, my friend, our jungle, and we know it like the back of our hand.'

They trekked for about an hour. It was hard to keep track of their direction in the densely shaded vegetation. Danny just had to put his faith in Tia and the others as they moved forever downhill towards the estate and the sea.

Danny heard the sound of a truck's engine labouring at low revs as it approached on an uneven track. Tia put her hand up before rolling around behind a large tree trunk. Danny flattened himself into the undergrowth next to Edgar, while Samuel and Miguel did the same a few metres to their right. Some thirty metres to their left, they could just make out the canvased side of a truck crawling into view along a muddy overgrown track. Diesel smoke chugged out the back as it revved, spinning the wheels to get a grip and move forward. It stopped directly ahead of them. Felipe jumped down from the cab, banging the side panels as he walked along the truck to the rear. He lowered the tailboard and eight of Delgado's armed soldiers jumped down. They listened to Felipe giving orders before spreading out along the track, turning into the rainforest and heading in their direction. Edgar was already lining up the sights on his M-16 when Danny leant over.

'No noise. If we can get past them to the truck, we can drive it straight into Delgado's estate.'

Edgar looked at Danny and nodded before crawling over to Samuel, Miguel, and Tia to tell them the plan. Seconds later they pushed their backpacks into the undergrowth ahead of them, burying themselves into ferns, tree saplings, and leafy debris, disappearing from sight before Danny's eyes. Following suit, Danny slid under the densest vegetation he could find, burying his face into the damp earth to hide his white skin. He pulled the razor-sharp hunting knife out of its sheath and slid it under the leafy soil to hide its glinting blade. Slowing his breathing, he remained absolutely still.

It wasn't long before he heard the telltale sounds of approaching boots, twigs snapping, the rustling drag of arms pushing vegetation aside. At that point Danny felt movement across his leg. It was light and slid agilely up across his buttocks before moving across his back. Fighting the urge to freak out and shake it off, Danny froze, holding his breath. With his head half buried in the dirt and only one eye visible, he felt the snake slide over his shoulder. The head appearing in his field of vision first, its black tongue flicking in and out as it tasted the scent of his sweat in the air. It moved half of its body off him onto the ground in front and curled around to face him, its head held a few inches off the ground as its golden eyes looked straight into his. Under the leaves and dirt, Danny gripped the knife tighter, conscious of the sound of the approaching soldier. He identified the snake by the shape of its head and markings as a venomous viper, possibly the fer-de-lance or common lancehead. One bite out here, miles from a hospital, would cause serious internal bleeding and a painful death.

Come on, on your way, mate. Jesus, if he sees me I'm dead; if you bite me I'm dead. Talk about being caught between a rock and a hard place.

The snake reared up, clearly agitated by the approaching soldier, but still focused on his face. Danny's whole body tensed, ready to whip the razor-sharp hunting knife at the snake if it tried to strike him. Twigs snapping a few feet away finally caused the snake to turn its head and move away, the soldier's rustling footsteps sounding dangerously close to Danny's ear. They moved away quickly as the soldier shouted, "*Cuidado serpiente!*" to warn the others of snakes.

Danny stayed absolutely still, holding his breath, his lungs burning for a few more minutes until the sound of Delgado's men faded away. Finally he breathed out before sucking great gulps of air, relieved not to be bitten or shot. Emerging from cover he kept low and joined the others as they headed stealthily through the cover of the rainforest towards the truck.

THIRTY TWO

Delgado entered the campaign headquarters to rapturous applause. Balloons and banners were strewn everywhere as the screens displayed the very first votes next to the three candidates' names.

'Thank you, everyone. Your support means everything to me. Let us hope that this time tomorrow the people of Colombia will have spoken with their votes, and that I, Balthasar Delgado, am your new President,' Delgado said, giving his best politician smile as he shook hands.

As soon as he could break away he moved over to Garcia. 'Tell me,' he demanded, the smile instantly gone.

'Felipe has dropped the men off. He's heading back to the estate to keep an eye on Mr Miller as the votes come in.'

'Very good. I want to know as soon as Pearson and the others are dead, the very second. Ok, Diego?'

'Si Señor.'

Delgado turned away from Garcia and, like flicking on a light switch, his face changed back to the one the public saw as he mingled with his supporters.

***

'Ok, let's get back,' Felipe ordered the driver.

'Si Señor Torres.'

Starting the truck up, the driver lurched it forward, yanking on the steering wheel to send it off the dirt track. It cracked and scraped its way forward through the undergrowth before he jammed it in reverse and pulled it back onto the track to face the way they'd come from. A heavy thump in the back made the driver pull to a stop. Felipe and the driver both looked at each other before looking in the mirrors at the sides of the truck. Everything looked as it should.

'You go to that side,' Felipe said, both of them pulling handguns before opening the doors to take another cautious glance down the side of the truck to the rear.

They jumped down into the mud, Felipe crouching to check under the chassis. Seeing it clear, he stood up and squelched his way down the side, his gun pointed at the canvas-topped flatbed that gave nothing away as to the source of the thumps. He reached the rear corner, flattening himself against the body of the truck before swinging around with his gun pointed. In a mirror image, the driver spun around from the other side, both men pointing their guns into empty space. They turned to face the tailboard, tentatively reaching in with a hand to grab a corner of the canvas flap that hid what lay inside. While pointing their guns in readiness, Felipe nodded to the driver and mouthed a count to three. His mouth had just formed the shape of three when the cold metal of gun muzzles pushed into the base of their skulls. Both men froze and put their guns passively up in the air. Danny and Tia reached forward and took them. The canvas flap opened in front of them to expose Edgar, Samuel, and Miguel's grinning faces behind their pointing rifles.

'You are all dead men,' Felipe said defiantly.

'Yeah, yeah, where have I heard that before?' Danny said, checking out the size of the driver. 'You, in the truck and strip. What do you reckon, Miguel? He's about your size, isn't he? Put the driver's clothes on and come up front.'

'If you piss your pants, I'm going to kill you, understand?' Miguel said, pulling the scared driver's baseball cap off his head.

While Miguel and Edgar pulled the driver into the back, Tia and Danny frog-marched Felipe back to the cab. Tia got in first, checking out the space behind the seats. It was big enough for Danny and Tia to squeeze into. Tia went first, kneeling behind the passenger seat. Danny pushed felipe up and sat him down, letting Tia cover him while he went around and climbed in from the driver's side. It was more of a struggle due to his size, but he managed to get down below the seat height with a clear angle to shoot Felipe if he tried anything. A few moments later, Miguel climbed in, dressed as the driver. He slammed the door and started driving the truck along the slippery dirt track towards the estate.

'There's a hundred men at the estate. You'll never get inside,' Felipe said with contempt.

'First, that's bullshit. The estate isn't that big, and I didn't see any accommodation blocks when we flew over, and second, most of the men you have are back there in the jungle looking for us. I bet there aren't more than half a dozen men at the estate.'

Felipe didn't answer Danny, he just sat still, looking out the front window.

'Road block up ahead,' Miguel said, pulling the baseball cap down low to hide his face.

'Tell them to let us through or I'll shoot you and them.'

Felipe didn't need to tell them. The sight of him in the passenger seat made the men jump to attention and push down on the counterweighted barrier to raise it out of the way. After another few minutes of bouncing around, with Danny cursing being squashed up behind the seat, the communication tower that loomed over the estate came into view. With the airstrip in sight at the end of the track, the truck hit a massive pothole, throwing them all to one side. Felipe took advantage of the shift and pushed the passenger door open, rolling out the side of the truck before Danny could grab him. He was on his feet and heading into the rainforest in a flash.

'Shit, I'll get him,' Danny yelled, unravelling himself from behind the drivers seat.

Gripping his handgun, Danny threw himself between the seats, falling out the still-swinging passenger door to roll up onto his feet. He ran full pelt after Felipe, zigzagging through the trees, following the sound of crunching and snapping twigs, his eyes picking out the movement of disturbed undergrowth as it attempted to settle back into position in the wake of Felipe. A log, swung like a baseball bat, appeared from behind a tree, striking Danny mid-chest as he ran forward. The impact knocking him clean off his feet as all the air left his lungs, his handgun firing into the air as it left his grip.

Stunned, Danny sucked air back into his lungs, focusing on Felipe as he spun from behind the tree. Raising the log above his head, Felipe drove it down towards Danny's skull. Rolling to one side, Danny swiped Felip's leg with a powerful kick to the side of his knee. Felipe's leg folded and the log thumped into the leafy forest floor inches from Danny's head. Rolling to the side, Danny grabbed the log and planted a boot into Felipe's face as he fell to his knee. The blow whipped Felipe's head back, his body following the momentum, sending him onto his back.

Both men dragged themselves upright. Felipe picked something shiny up in the undergrowth next to him. Realising it was his gun, Danny exploded forward. He grabbed Felipe's wrist with one hand while ramming his other around Felipe's throat, gripping it like a vice. Shots rang out to the shrieks of startled monkeys and panicked birds. With his free hand, Felipe started powering punches into Danny's side until the grip on his neck loosened. Another blow and Danny released his hand to protect his side. Felipe grabbed Danny's other arm, slowly twisting it as Danny tried desperately, and failed, to keep the gun from moving towards his head. Reaching down, Danny found the hunting knife in its sheath. Shaking from the exertion and with the muscles in his arm screaming, Danny pulled the knife out of the sheath, thrusting it up under Felipe's chin. He pushed it harder, not stopping until the blade disappeared up to the hilt. Felipe's body went limp, leaving him hanging on Danny's shaking arm until he let him fall to the ground. Breathing heavily, Danny pulled the knife out and picked up his gun. He wiped the knife blade on Felipe's dead body, then turned slowly and headed back to the truck.

THIRTY THREE

'Nothing?' Rico shouted to the approaching soldiers.

'No, nothing,' the man replied, moving up to join Rico's men.

Rico turned to see the last of Felipe's men emerging from the forest. They shook their heads at him.

'Perhaps they went away from the estate, north, towards the river.'

'No, this man, Pearson, he will not give up on his friend,' Rico said, turning his head at the sound of a gunshot. Everyone froze, looking to the south to see birds rising from the treetops near the estate. Two more shots rang out, snapping Rico into action.

'In the truck, now,' he shouted, running toward the vehicle. 'What's happening?' he yelled into the radio as he jumped into the passenger seat.

'I don't know. Felipe came through in the truck, then we heard shots somewhere near the airfield. We're heading that way now,' came the voice from the sentry on the roadblock.

'Call me as soon as you find something,' Rico said impatiently. 'Felipe, where are you? We're on our way back. Come in, Felipe.'

He waited, listening to empty static as the last man got in the back of the truck and it moved off, rumbling along the bumpy track as fast as it could.

'Felipe, come in, Felipe. Get this tub of crap moving faster, now,' Rico shouted at the driver.

Frightened that Rico might shoot him and drive the truck himself, the driver put his foot down. The truck lurched forward, bouncing precariously through the trees, leaving the soldiers in the back once again holding on for dear life.

A short time later they barrelled through the open roadblock, stopping further down the track where Felipe had jumped out earlier. The sentry guards from the roadblock appeared at the sound of the approaching truck and flagged them down.

'What is it?' Rico shouted out of the window.

'Señor Torres, it's your brother.' Their eyes fell to the ground, and they bowed their heads in respect of the dead.

'My brother, where is he?' Rico demanded, jumping down from the truck.

'He is over here, I am sorry, Señor Torres, Felipe is dead,' one of the men said, leading Rico into the trees.

When they came to Felipe's blood-soaked body, Rico fell to his knees next to his twin. He remained there staring at his brother until his eyes narrowed and the muscles in his jaw tensed as his anger grew.

'You two, take my brother and put him in the back of the truck,' he said, standing up and marching away, leaving them to carry the body.

Rico climbed back into the passenger seat and sat in silence, staring out the front windscreen. The driver sat in silence too, not daring to speak until Rico gave him his next command. Looking in the wing mirror, he saw the two men carry Felipe's body around to the rear of the truck. A few seconds later he felt the truck rock as they put him in the back and climbed in. Two knocks on the back of the cab signalled they were ready to go.

'Drive,' Rico said, pulling the two handguns from his shoulder holsters to hold them in his lap, ready for action.

THIRTY FOUR

They burst out of the cover of the forest onto the airfield, mud spinning off the tyres as Miguel turned the truck towards the gates of the estate. As they came around, Danny opened fire with the M-16 rifle, his legs spread inside the cab to stop him falling out as his head and torso hung out the window to fire. Caught by surprise, the two men on the gate gave up any thoughts of firing back and dived for cover as bullets thumped into the heavy wooden gate.

'Just drive straight through it, go, go, go!' Danny yelled to Miguel.

Miguel floored the accelerator and the lumbering truck started to gain speed. It struck the gate dead centre, snapping the locking bar on the back into splintered pieces as it burst through. Cornering off the drive, Miguel ploughed a trough across the lawn, straight towards the pool terrace. Automatic fire from behind them made Danny turn his head. The two men from the gate flailed around, one of them firing into the air as he jerked and fell to the floor, cut down by Edgar and Samuel's shots from out the back of the truck.

The truck stopped abruptly when the front hit the low wall around the pool terrace, sending bricks and ornate flower pots splashing into the pool. Danny and Miguel leaped out fast, kneeling down behind the wall with guns aimed over the top at the large patio doors. Seconds later, Tia, Edgar, and Samuel were out to join them.

'Keep down,' Danny shouted, tapping a few rounds at one of Delgado's soldiers as he poked his head out the doors, driving him back inside.

'Let's go,' Edgar said.

'No, no, wait. Miguel, can you and Samuel take that communication tower out with the dynamite?'

'Yeah, I guess, if we pack it around one of the support legs.'

'Good. Go and do it. It'll stop Delgado's men communicating and make it hard for them to organise a search party once we get out of here.'

'What about the house?'

'We'll deal with the house. You blow the tower and meet us inside.'

Miguel and Samuel scooted off around the low wall and headed towards the rear of the house.

'Ok, you two cover me while I go in, then I'll cover you while you join me. That's how it goes. You cover, I move, you join, OK?'

'Ok, we've got it,' Tia said, eager to get on and find her husband.

Danny nodded and shuffled along to the steps up to

the terrace while Tia and Edgar looked down their rifle sights for movement in the house. After taking a few deep breaths, Danny tensed his legs, focused on the house, then released. He powered around the pool, his rifle tucked into his shoulder as he looked down the sights. Ducking into a large dining room, Danny folded himself flat against the wall next to the doorway to the hall. He looked back at Tia and Edgar and signalled for them to join him. While they headed around the pool, Danny shot a glance into the hall, pulling back sharply as Arvin took potshots at his head. The bullets tore into the door frame, sending razor sharp splinters into the room. Propping the M-16 rifle against the wall, Danny pulled the two handguns out of the back of his trouser belt. He counted to three and dived into the doorway at ground level, locking both arms with guns out in front of him.

Arvin was still aiming with shaky hands at head height and empty space. By the time he'd seen his low dive, Danny had double-tapped both triggers, sending bullets into centre mass, blowing Arvin into the wall on the far side of the hall. As Arvin slid slowly down the wall to slump on the floor, Danny popped back up to his feet. He entered the hall, his eyes and guns moving in unison as they covered ahead and up the twin sweeping staircases.

'Ground floor first,' Danny said as Tia and Edgar appeared beside him.

Danny moved past the staircases and turned down a corridor, Tia and Edgar covering the side doors and rear as he went. A man appeared at the far end pulling a door shut behind him before he turned and raised his gun. Danny was ahead of him, shooting him in the shoulder before he'd levelled his gun. It clattered to the ground as the man fell clutching the wound. They moved over to him as he writhed on the floor in agony, Edgar covering him with his rifle while Danny turned his attention to the door he came out of. Tucking a gun into his belt so he could grip the door handle, Danny prepared to enter, holding his other gun ready to shoot any hostiles inside.

Ok, one, two, three.

He yanked the handle down and pushed the door open as fast as he could.

THIRTY FIVE

'Did you hear that, old man? What the hell's going on out there?' said Scott at the sound of gunfire and a boom as the gate splintered apart.

When more gunfire echoed from somewhere inside the house, Scott turned away from the rising election figures to look at Luis. Both of them sat motionless, not knowing what they should do. The sound of gunfire got louder and approaching footsteps made them look to the door in trepidation. They both jumped when it shot open to reveal a wide-eyed Quinto holding a handgun.

'Stay here and don't come out,' he shouted, pulling the door shut again.

'Where's my sister?' Scott shouted after him.

'I wonder what is going on,' Luis said.

'Well, I think we're about to find—' Scott paused when gunfire echoed in the corridor outside, followed by a groan of pain. 'Out,' Scott said, finishing his sentence.

The door flew open before Luis could answer, a handgun appearing first before Danny's head followed it. Quinto was on the floor in the corridor, groaning in agony as he held his hand to the bullet wound in his shoulder.

'Good afternoon, Daniel, nice of you to join us. Would you mind asking our friend on the floor what room they're holding Nikki in?' Scott said with a smile.

'What, Nikki? She's here? How?' Danny said, surprised.

Before he could answer, Tia put her head around the door, the relief showing as she caught sight of her husband. She pushed past Danny and hugged Luis tightly, tears rolling down her cheeks.

'Yes, they flew her in yesterday,' Scott said, continuing.

Scott barely got the last word out before Danny turned back into the corridor, dropped to the floor, and grabbed Quinto. Ignoring his screaming, Danny dug his thumb into the bullet wound.

'Where is she?' he growled, releasing the pressure on his shoulder.

'She's not here. Delgado took her with him.' Quinto grunted out the answer, gulping breaths to talk through the pain.

'Took her where?' Danny growled, pulling his arm back to punch Quinto mercilessly in the shoulder, then bringing his bloodied fist back, ready for another punch.

'No, no, don't. Bogotá, he took her back to his house in Bogotá,' Quinto pleaded through gritted teeth.

'Fuck,' Danny yelled, punching Quinto squarely between the eyes in frustrated fury, knocking him clean out. 'Time to go,' he said after a few seconds, his mood still dark but emotions back in control.

'Hang on, I just need to do something,' Scott said, rapidly opening windows on the computer screens while typing furiously on the keyboard.

Before Danny could protest, there was a massive explosion at the back of the estate. Samuel and Miguel had dynamited the support legs of the communications tower. An eerie silence followed the explosion. Metallic screeches and clangs quickly replaced the silence as the stress on the remaining supports caused them to fold and collapse. The tower fell away from the house, crashing into the solar panels with an ear shattering boom. A shower of glass crystals catapulted high into the air before raining back down onto the wreckage.

'Oh my lord, what have you done?' Scott said, panicking at the lost signal message blinking on the multiple screens.

'We've taken out their comms, mate. It'll leave them blind while we make our escape, and they won't be able to contact Delgado and tell him what's going on. Leave it, Scott, come on, it's time to go,' Danny said, puzzled by Scott's reaction.

'No, you don't understand. I programmed a surprise for Delgado. When the last votes are counted and the clock hits midnight, my program will kick in. The results screen will display the real vote and the fake one side by side. Sixty seconds later, a mass of incriminating documents I hacked from Delgado's computer will scroll across the results screen. All the news feeds will broadcast it right across Colombia, and the rest of the world for that matter. Delgado will know it was me who set him up and take revenge on Nikki for sure.'

'Oh for fuck's sake, can you stop it, Scott? Buy us more time?' Danny asked.

'That, dear boy, was precisely what I was doing right before you blew up the internet feed. So no, I can't stop it.'

'Shit, ok, first things first we get the hell out of here. Then we'll figure out how to get back to Bogotá before midnight and get Nikki back,' Danny said.

The sound of people approaching stopped the conversation. Danny and Edgar spun their guns around, relieved to see it was only Samuel and Miguel.

'Time to go, bro, we've got company,' said Samuel.

They moved out towards the dining room, heading towards the patio doors to the pool terrace. Danny handed his gun to Scott and picked up the M-16 he left propped against the wall earlier. Taking the lead, Danny entered the dining room and looked out of the patio windows at the pool and gardens beyond. His eyes went wide and he dived back behind a heavy sideboard. The large expanse of bi-folding patio doors exploded inwards, filling the room from one side to the other in millions of twinkling glass crystals. The noise was ear shattering. Bullets ripped through the crockery along the centre of the dining table, embedding themselves into the wall opposite. Little clouds of plaster dust popped into the air. When the volley of fire finished, Danny shook the glass out of his unruly hair. He rolled out from behind the sideboard and fired short bursts back at Rico and his men tucked behind the estate wall. It kept them behind cover for a few seconds before heads and guns reappeared over the top of the wall, and another hail of bullets ripped the room apart.

'Back. We've got to find another way,' Danny yelled over the noise as he front crawled back into the hall.

'How are we going to get out?' Edgar said.

'Er, hang on, let me think,' Danny said, looking through the small window next to the front door.

Rico and the soldiers were moving to the gate ready to storm the house.

'Well, while you're making your head hurt, Daniel, if everyone would like to follow me, there is another way out. Over here please,' Scott said, waving them over as he headed for the door to the wine cellar under the stairs and opened it.

'Scott, what the fuck are you doing? We lock ourselves in a cellar and we sign our own death warrant.'

'Oh, I don't think so, dear boy, come along and I'll show you,' Scott said with a certain amount of smugness.

They all made their way down the steps with Danny following reluctantly behind them. Danny rolled his eyes when he got to the bottom and discovered they were standing in a large square wine cellar with no way out.

'For fuck's sake, Scott, Danny said, turning to go back up the stairs.

He got one foot on the bottom step when he heard the creak and squeaking sound of the wheel on the bottom of the heavy door rolling on the stone floor. Turning back, Danny caught Scott's smile and the long tunnel leading into the distance beside him.

'This way, people. Daniel, be a good fellow and shut the door on your way through,' said Scott, leading the way.

Danny looked at the door before closing it. Moving back into the wine cellar, he pulled some of the wooden slats out that the bottles slid into position on. Pushing the door shut, he wedged the wooden slats into the narrow gap between the bottom and the stone floor, kicking them until they were firmly wedged in position.

THIRTY SIX

'You men, move up behind the truck,' Rico ordered, pointing to the crashed vehicle by the pool terrace.

The men looked at him sheepishly before psyching themselves up and running for the truck, the fear of what Rico would do if they disobeyed outweighing the fear of getting shot by Danny and his people in the house. They reached the truck without a shot being fired. Out of habit, Rico tried to talk to them on the radio once they were in position. He threw it on the floor in a rage when he realised it was a fruitless task with the communications tower gone. He pulled his phone out in the slim chance he might get enough signal to call Delgado. It looked back at him without a single signal bar on its display.

'His death will be slow and painful, I swear it. I will make him pay, Felipe,' Rico muttered, looking back at the truck with his twin brother's body lying in the back. 'Let's move.'

On Rico's command they stormed through the

broken gates and ran for the house, tucking in behind the low wall to the pool terrace. No shots or movement came from the house. Rico split the men and went in through the glassless patio doors. The others headed in through the front door and into the kitchen on the far side of the house. They moved slowly through the house, sweeping each room as they went. It was all quiet apart from the sound of crunching glass underfoot, a pain-filled groan echoed from the corridor towards the rear of the house. With both handguns up ahead of him, Rico moved into the hall and turned towards the groaning sound. He saw Arvin dead against the wall. A noise made Rico's group spin, holding off on firing when the rest of his men appeared from the kitchen.

'Search upstairs,' Rico said, while waving to the others to follow him.

He walked past the twin staircases, following the sound. Darting his head into the corridor at the back of the house, he saw Quinto. He'd dragged himself into a sitting position, propped up against the wall, his hand pressed on the bullet wound to stem the bleeding.

'How many of them?' Rico said, his voice cold, with no hint of concern for Quinto's injury.

'Five, the man Pearson, Rojas's wife and three others,' Quinto said through grunts of pain.

'Where did they go?'

'I don't know. I heard all the shooting, then the house went quiet. Rico, I need a hospital, please.'

Rico looked down at him. His expression remained emotionless as he raised his gun to Quinto's head.

'Rico, no, Rico.'

The gunshot echoed along the corridor. His men came running, guns up and ready. They stopped short and moved away silently at the sight of Rico standing over Quinto's body. None of them daring to question Rico's actions.

'Well? Where are they?' Rico shouted as he walked back into the hallway.

The men returned from their search upstairs shaking their heads. Rico stood in the middle of the two staircases deep in thought. After a few moments he turned slowly to face the door to the wine cellar.

'They're heading for the cave. You men follow me, the rest of you go in through the hangar and cut them off. Move,' he shouted, pulling the door open.

Moving cautiously down the stairs to the wine cellar, Rico headed for the hidden door to the tunnel. He pulled on the bottle to release the latch. Nothing happened. The door remained firmly shut. Rico pushed on the section of rack that should have opened. He could feel the top flex inwards slightly, but the bottom didn't budge.

'Give me that,' he said, putting his handguns back into their holsters to take an M-16 rifle off one of the men. 'Get back.'

They all did as he said. Rico flicked the rifle into fully automatic and fired at the bottom of the door. He didn't flinch as glass, wine rack and bits of the door flew around him. The bottom of the door eventually disintegrated, swinging inwards as the rifle clicked empty. He handed the rifle back, drew his own guns, and marched into the tunnel ahead of his men.

THIRTY SEVEN

'Here they come, guys,' Danny said, hearing the echoing gunfire from way back behind him.

'We're nearly there,' Scott said, descending the last of the steps before the tunnel entered the cave.

'Nearly where, Scott? What's down h—' Danny said, stumped for words when they came out into a massive cave.

'Delgado's using a submarine to smuggle his cocaine. It was here the other day. It must be off running cocaine up the coast to the States. The perfect way to move his product. Surface off the coast of Florida next to a fishing boat for the exchange. Well, something along those lines anyway,' Scott said, rather pleased with himself. He pointed out the pallets on the dock, one stacked with plastic-wrapped blocks of dollar bills, the other with cocaine bricks.

'Yep, very impressive, Scott, but if you don't mind, we've got more pressing things to deal with,' Danny said, running past them to hop into the forklift.

'Er, yes, sorry, of course. This way, everyone, we can get out up that slope over there. It leads to the hangar on the airstrip.'

While the others moved along the quay, Danny spun the forklift around and lifted the six-feet high pallet of cocaine bricks. He drove it back to the tunnel entrance. Shouts and gunfire sounded from within as he straightened up. Little puffs of cocaine dust appeared above the stack as bullets hit the cocaine bricks on the other side. Danny drove the load and forklift forward, wedging it hard against the tunnel entrance, sealing it off from the cave, muffling the noise into silence.

That should keep them busy for a while.

Joining the others on the far side, Danny moved over to Edgar as he stared at the pallet loaded with millions of dollars' worth of plastic-wrapped bills.

'Sorry, my friend, we're going to have enough trouble getting out of here alive without trying to carry the money as well,' Danny said, patting him on the back.

Edgar tore himself away to look at Danny and nod his agreement before hopping up onto the concrete and rock slope with the others. They followed it up out of the cave into a large tunnel blasted into the rock. The interior was lit by a row of bulkheads fixed every five metres to the side of the rock.

'They bring the trucks down this way. I've seen them. They unload the cocaine before spinning the truck around on the turning plate thingy at the bottom. The truck then drives back up here to the hangar by the airstrip,' Scott said, trying to see the end of the tunnel in the darkness ahead.

The whine of electric motors up ahead caused them to stop and raise their weapons.

'I don't like the sound of that,' Edgar said, as a slither of light illuminated the end of the cave ahead of them. The floor of the hangar above started lowering on two large hydraulic arms. Legs, rifle muzzles and hands—and a lot of them—appeared on the lowering truck ramp.

'Back down the tunnel, now,' Danny said, jogging backwards as the other went ahead, his guns trained on the ever-widening gap.

Delgado's men squatted down to see down the tunnel before the platform fully lowered. They saw Danny in the distance and fired. Thankfully their position made it impossible to aim properly. Danny dropped a few of them while he retreated with bullets flying past him high and wide.

'Miguel, have you got any dynamite left?' Danny shouted, running out of the tunnel and into the cave.

'Yes, I have a couple of sticks,' Miguel answered, swinging the rucksack off his back.

'Then fucking throw them up the tunnel and make it quick.'

'It won't do much damage unless it's buried in the rock,' Miguel said, holding the two sticks while lighting the fuse wire.

'It'll keep them back while I think,' Danny said, leaving Miguel jumping back up onto the ramp.

He hurled the dynamite as far up the cave as he

could, turning fast to jump away as a hail of bullets whizzed past him. The fuse wire was only long enough for a few seconds but it felt like minutes until the dynamite exploded, deafening in the confines of the cave.

Shit, think, how are we going to get out of this one?

The shards of light cutting their way through the water from the underwater tunnel to the outside gave him the answer.

'We'll have to swim for it, underwater, out of the mouth of the cave.'

'Are you sure, old boy? We don't know how far it is. We could drown,' Scott said, staring at the light patch of water, frowning.

'Judging by the amount of sunlight coming in it can't be too far, besides it's either that or be shot, and I know which one I prefer,' Danny said, jamming his handguns into the back of his trousers, before stripping off his rucksack and jacket.

With no time to think about the choices, the others did the same, following Danny as he ran to the end of the jetty and dived into the water. They swam up to the rock face with the light from outside the cave dancing below their feet. Danny was about to say he'd go first to check out how far it was when Delgado's men poured out of the truck tunnel, shouting and firing wildly in their direction.

'Go, go, quickly,' Danny said, taking a deep breath before diving under the water.

He swam down into the tunnel out of the cave, his

eyes open, the vision very blurred without goggles. He headed towards the source of the sunlight as bullets tore lines through the water beside him like spears disappearing into the deep. Samuel was the last man to dive below the surface. He'd got a couple of metres down when a bullet tore through the flesh on the side of his thigh, the pain and shock making him panic and swim erratically into the mouth of the tunnel. Unable to swim efficiently, and with his adrenaline levels through the roof, Samuel's body burned through the air in his lungs in no time. Confused and scared, he swam upwards, banging his head on the tunnel roof. Panicking, he scraped his hands on the rock surface, trying to pull himself along as his lungs screamed for air. His movements slowed until he convulsed a few times and fell still. He floated away from the rock with his eyes open, staring at the blurred images of Danny and the rest of his family swimming away.

THIRTY EIGHT

'Get this shit out of the way,' Rico demanded as his men tried to pull one of the tightly packed cocaine bricks from the pallet wall blocking their exit.

'Idiots, out the fucking way,' Rico shouted, taking the rifle off the man beside him, immediately emptying the magazine into a small square of cocaine bricks.

Everyone flattened themselves against the wall of the tunnel, their hands over their ears, trying to muffle the ear-shattering noise in the confined space. The gun clicked empty as cocaine bricks shattered back into powder, filling the air in a white haze.

'Don't just stand there, pull them out,' Rico shouted, throwing the empty rifle on the floor and kicking the backsides of the men to get them moving.

They worked frantically, pulling the blown-apart cocaine bricks out, allowing them to work the other bricks loose and pull them out. They eventually freed enough bricks to see the inside of the cave through the top of the stack.

'Out of the way,' Rico growled, pushing his way through them to the front. 'Hey, over here.'

There was a tense silence for a few moments which had everyone inside the tunnel worried Rico would explode at any minute and shoot them all.

'I'm here, Señor Torres,' came a response as a man climbed up onto the stack of cocaine to look through the gap.

'Get me out of here now,' Rico said through gritted teeth.

The man jumped off the top and climbed into the forklift, reversing the load out of the way as quickly as he could. Rico stormed into the cave the second it was clear, followed by the men behind him.

'Where are they?' he yelled, his face flushed with anger.

'They swam out of the cave, Señor Torres.'

Rico ran to the end of the jetty drawing his two handguns to lock them up in front of him. He scanned the water, emptying both magazines into the red trail of Samuel's blood as it disappeared into the mouth of the tunnel.

'You two, go in after them,' Rico shouted at the top of his voice to the two men nearest him.

They looked back apprehensively but still dropped their rifles on the deck and pulled their commando knives out. Watching Rico's face, they moved nervously to the edge of the dock.

'Hurry up, or I'll shoot you myself,' Rico growled, intimidating the two men by sliding a fresh magazine into his gun and pulling the slide back to chamber a round, his eyes never leaving them.

Knowing Rico would shoot them in a heartbeat, the two men dived in the water and swam towards the rock face.

'Up to the hangar. Now. Move. We need to head them off at the bottom of the cliff,' Rico yelled, running ahead of his men.

Spurred on by the need to avenge his brother's death, Rico jumped up onto the truck ramp and powered up into the tunnel. He jumped over the rock debris from the dynamite explosion, his men trying to keep up with him as he headed into the hangar.

THIRTY NINE

Danny surfaced first, spinning around in the water to see the jetty, speed boat and seaplane twenty metres to his left. He turned again at the sound of Tia and Luis surfacing seconds before Edgar and Miguel. The relief to be out of the cave was immediately replaced by concern when Samuel didn't surface.

'Get to the jetty, I'll go back for him,' Danny shouted.

He took a few deep breaths and dived back down before the others could say anything. Using long, powerful strokes with his arms and legs, Danny glided quickly through the water. He homed in on the blurred image of Samuel as he floated lifelessly in the tunnel. Danny grabbed Samuel under the arm and turned to swim him back out, surprised to see Edgar appear beside him to grab Samuel's other arm. As they headed towards the sunlight coming in from open water, a hand grabbed Danny's ankle and wrenched him back away from Edgar and Samuel. Danny kicked back hard with his free leg, the heel of his boot connecting hard with the nose of one of Delgado's men. The man recoiled in a cloud of bubbles as he released his breath.

Letting go of Danny's ankle, he put his hands to his face and swam back towards the cave, desperate for air. Before Danny could turn and swim after Edgar, a second man appeared from behind his fleeing colleague. Even through the blurred vision, Danny could see the glints of reflected sunlight off a razor-sharp commando knife. Choosing to float motionless, Danny fought the ever-increasing burning feeling in his lungs and put all his focus on the approaching man's knife hand. When he made the lunge forward, thrusting the knife at his torso, Danny twisted out the way, catching the man's wrist as the knife sliced into empty water. Jamming his other hand into the man's throat, Danny kicked and pushed them upward, crunching the side of the guy's face into the roof of the tunnel. Kicking hard, Danny dragged the side of his face across the surface, the sharp rock tearing lumps out of his cheek as puffs of red blood bloomed in the water. He thrashed around, trying to get free, the panic burning up what little air he had left.

Keeping calm, even though his body screamed for him to get air, Danny let go of the man's neck. Grabbing his knife arm with a second hand, Danny twisted and pushed the blade up with all the strength he had left. The man's mouth opened to emit a silent scream of bubbles as the knife sliced into his belly up to the handle. Pulling the knife out in a cloud of red blood, Danny pushed the convulsing man away.

Turning, he swam back out of the underwater tunnel,

his head spinning and lungs burning. He broke the surface, taking a minute to suck in great gulps of air before spinning to face the jetty. Edgar had got Samuel out and was performing CPR on the wooden walkway while the others watched, no one daring to say a word. As Miguel and Scott pulled Danny up out of the water, Samuel's body jerked and he drew in a massive breath of air. He turned on his side and threw up sea water before breathing heavily.

'Welcome back to the land of the living. Sorry to hurry you, but any second now a load of very angry men are going to come down that cliff after us. I suggest we get into that speed boat and get the hell out of here,' Danny said urgently.

He looked across at the seaplane and shook his head as they moved to the boat.

'Damn, I wish I knew how to fly. I could be in Bogotá before the final votes are counted.'

'I can fly us,' Scott said, his head poking out from behind Edgar.

'What, since when?' Danny said, raising his eyebrows in surprise.

'New hobby, old man, I've been taking lessons. I thought I might get myself a little runabout for weekends in France and that sort of thing.'

'Ok, ok, stop talking and get in the bloody plane,' Danny said, jumping onto the plane's skid to open the door.

'Alright, no need to be rude,' Scott said, hopping across to get in.

'Do you need us to come with you?' Edgar said.

'No, you take the boat, get your family home, and Edgar?'

'Yes?'

'Thank you all for everything,' Danny said with a smile.

'No, thank you for everything, my friend,' Edgar said, extending a hand to Danny.

Danny shook it, and both men parted. He cut the moorings with the commando knife and climbed into the plane beside Scott. Edgar and his family fired up the speedboat, pushed the throttle to max and took off up the coast.

'Ok, let's go, Scotty boy,' Danny said, slamming the door shut beside him.

'Er, yes, quite, let's go. Er…' Scott dithered as he tapped the dials and twister control knobs.

'Scott, you do know how to fly this?'

'Of course, I'm just familiarising myself with the controls. Mmm, yes that should be it,' he said, pressing a red button to his left.

The propeller whined as it spun. A clunky banging sound preceded a big puff of black smoke from the exhaust before the engine caught and fired into life. At the very same moment, bullets tore shards of wood off the jetty and splashes of water danced up beside the plane.

'Get us out of here now, Scott,' Danny shouted, ducking down low in his seat so he could see the cliff top.

Rico stood between a line of men at the top, his face a

picture of hate and anger as he shouted for his men to fire at the plane. Scott pushed the throttle forward. Between the surrounding splashes, a row of bullets caught their target. Holes ripped through the top of the plane behind them, punching through the passenger seats before ricocheting around the back. As they gained speed and moved out of range, the bullets splashed into empty water in their wake.

'Gosh, that was jolly exciting. Now let's see, flaps down, speed up a bit and…'

A huge grin spread across Scott's face as the plane bounced then skipped across the tops of the small waves before rising into the air.

As Scott gained altitude and turned the plane around to head over land, Danny looked out the side window. Edgar and the others in the speedboat were moving fast, disappearing out of sight of the estate as they powered around the rugged coastline.

'Right, Scotty boy, get us to Bogotá as fast as this tub of crap will take us.'

'Yes, right, here we go. Er, I don't suppose you know what direction that might be, do you?' Scott said, looking at him with a blank face.

'Jesus, Scott, how many lessons have you actually had?'

'Er, five. Well, four actually. The first one was just in the classroom,' Scott said sheepishly.

'I wish I hadn't asked. If I thought you could actually land this thing, I'd ask you to put me back down. I'll take my chances with Delgado's men,' Danny said, craning his neck to look back out the window at the estate. 'You do know what the direction compass looks like?'

'Don't be facetious, Daniel. Of course I do, and for your information, it's called a heading indicator, or a directional gyro,' Scott said, rolling his eyes.

Looking around the instrument panel, Scott pointed to a little glass display, the picture of a plane in its centre pointing out their direction on a rotating disc marked with compass degrees.

'Ok, on the plane down here the direction was 358 degrees. Take 180 degrees away from that and you have a direction of 178 degrees for the return journey,' Danny said, unable to contain a chuckle.

'That will be quite enough of that, thank you very much,' Scott replied, turning the plane until the compass sat on 178 degrees. 'So what's the plan?'

'Get back to Bogotá and get Nikki back before the vote count ends and your little surprise tips Delgado off that we're coming.'

Pulling the two handguns from his waistband, Danny frowned as seawater trickled out when he ejected the magazines.

'Sounds pretty simple,' Scott said, turning the plane's heater up to help dry his clothes.

'The simple ones are always the best,' Danny replied, looking around the plane.

He fished a rag out from under his seat and popped the bullets out of the magazine before stripping the guns into half a dozen pieces to clean them.

FORTY

Rico watched the plane go. He pulled his phone out again and stared at the no signal indicator for a few moments. Turning slowly, he looked at the empty sky where the communication tower used to be.

'They don't want us to contact Señor Delgado. Something is wrong.' He looked to the sky and watched the plane head south, disappearing out of sight over the mountains. 'They're going for Bogotá and the girl. You. Refuel the truck. I want it ready to go in five minutes.'

'Where are we going, Señor Torres?'

'To Santa Marta airport, I need to get cell service and warn Señor Delgado, then fly to Bogotá as quickly as possible.'

'It will take a few hours to get there, Señor Torres. It will be too dark to drive on the forest track soon. We should go in the morning at first light,' the man protested.

'Did I ask for your opinion?' Rico growled, raising his gun and blowing the man's brains out in front of the rest of the shocked men. 'You. Refuel the truck and have it ready to go in five minutes,' Rico said, turning to the nearest man standing beside the corpse.

'Si, Señor Torres,' he said, running off to refuel the truck as fast as his legs would carry him.

***

Delgado arrived at the city hall, the picture of a squeaky clean politician, smiling to the press as he moved his way into the grand hall, shaking hands and waving. He got up on stage with the other candidates, the large projected screen behind him displaying his lead in the campaign results.

'It would seem you are proving the polls wrong, Señor Delgado,' said a reporter, fighting his way over to Delgado.

'It is too early to start celebrating yet, my friend. There are still a couple of hours to go. But I have faith the right man will be in office tomorrow,' Delgado replied, his smile firmly locked in place. His eyes looked at Garcia, beckoning him from the other side of the room. 'Excuse me, I must talk with my colleague.'

He fought his way across the room, the smiles and waves dropping like a stone as he stepped into a quiet corridor next to Garcia.

'What is it?'

'I am unable to contact anyone at the estate,' Garcia said, his facial expression emotionally unreadable.

Delgado frowned, deep in thought. He turned and

looked into the hall at the projected display still showing him with Scott's programmed lead in the votes.

'It could be nothing, a comms error or power outage. We've had them before,' he said, turning back to Garcia.

'Yes señor, it could be,' Garcia said, unconvinced.

'Call the cell company in Santa Marta, see if there is a problem at their end.'

'Si señor.'

Delgado turned and headed back to the hall, turning at the doorway to look back at Garcia.

'Call the house. Have the woman cleaned and dressed. Something sexy. I intend to celebrate my presidency tonight. Before I kill her.'

'Si senor.'

The second Delgado disappeared, Garcia was on the phone to the cell company that supplied the link to the estate. He frowned when the supervisor told him their system was live, but he was getting no return ping from the estate's comms tower. With nothing he could do, and no way to get hold of the estate, Garcia did as his boss instructed. He called the house in Bogotá and told them to get Nikki ready to receive Delgado, then lock her in his bedroom.

FORTY ONE

'We've got civilisation below us, old man. Try it now,.' Scott said, looking down at the twinkling lights of a town below them.

'Do you think it'll work after being in seawater?' Danny said, holding the power on button on his phone.

'An iPhone XS should do. They're IP rated for something like thirty minutes underwater,' Scott replied, smiling when the Apple logo burst into life on the phone.

'Well that's a good sign anyway. Let's hope we can get some signal up here.'

'Just make sure you don't make a video call by mistake. It might get misconstrued and one has a reputation to uphold,' said Scott.

He looked down then across at both of them sitting in the pilot and co-pilot's seats in nothing more than their underpants, their clothes hanging over the passenger seats behind, drying.

'Shut up, you tart,' Danny said, chuckling.

'While you're walking around with your caveman

knuckles dragging on the floor, looking for the next person to punch, some of us have a very important image to maintain to very important clients.'

The next thing Scott knew, Danny spun around grinning before blinding him with the flash from his camera on the phone.

'You're such a child,' Scott said, trying his hardest not to grin back at his best friend.

'Oh, hang on, here we go. We've got a signal.'

'Why don't you stick it on maps and see where we are.'

Danny did as Scott said, shrinking the map down until he could see where they were and where Bogotá was.

'That's the town of Chiquinquirá below us, so we're off a bit. Swing us five degrees west, Scotty boy, and we should be bang on target. Half an hour, forty minutes away, something like that.'

Scott turned the plane a little before straightening up again.

'Who are you going to call? We don't speak Spanish and who'd believe us?'

'A US DEA agent me and Nikki went to see at the American Embassy when we arrived in Bogotá, Gabriel something. I put his office and mobile number in the contacts. Here it is, Gabriel Anderson.'

'Well, Daniel, I am impressed,' Scott said.

'Eh, impressed because I remembered him?' Danny said, puzzled.

'No, I'm impressed that you managed to put his details in your phone,' Scott said, a smirk crossing his face again.

Danny rolled his eyes and hit the call button, cursing when it rang six times before going to the answerphone.

'Hi this is United States DEA Agent Gabriel Anderson. Please leave your name, number and the nature of your enquiry. I'll get back to you as soon as possible.'

'Gabriel, this is Daniel Pearson. I came to see you a few days ago with Nikki Miller about the kidnap of our friend, Scott Miller. I've rescued Scott Miller and Tia and Luis Rojas. Balthasar Delgado kidnapped them and held them at his estate near Santa Marta. He made Scott and Luis Rojas hack into the election results computer and rig the outcome. Delgado got to Nikki Miller before I could get there, he's holding her at his house in Bogotá. If you get this, we need you to get the Colombian authorities to arrest Delgado and meet us at his Bogotá house.'

Danny sat very quiet, frowning at the little lit up screen until it faded to black. It was after eleven and the chances of Gabriel Anderson hearing that message before morning were slim.

'Don't worry, old man, we'll get her back,' Scott said softly, putting his hand on Danny's shoulder.

After a couple of seconds Danny looked down and then across at Scott in his pants. 'Might be a good idea to put some clothes on first, aye, mate.'

FORTY TWO

Facing her second night locked in the bedroom in Delgado's mansion, Nikki was still trying to find a way to escape. With sealed panels of toughened glass in the windows and an armed guard outside the locked door, she was coming up short on ideas.

Delgado had ignored her on the flight back from the coastal estate. He was busy working on his election speech while Garcia flicked a knife open and told her he would gut her if she dared speak again. The only people she'd seen since she arrived were the housemaid and the guard from outside the door. He followed the maid in when she brought her food and drink, then stood leering at her until she'd eaten. Shouting for the maid to take the empty plate away, he made sure Nikki hadn't slipped a knife or fork from the tray. Following the maid out, the guard slammed the door shut behind them, the sound of the key turning in the lock dampening Nikki's spirits.

She gave up on the windows and walked into the en-suite bathroom, looking into the mirror screwed tightly to the wall above the sink. A tired reflection of herself looked back, her eyes puffy from the tears of an earlier low moment. But now she was angry. She looked at the towels next to the bath and picked them up, thinking. Opening them up across the sink, Nikki walked back into the bedroom. Grabbing a pillow off the bed, she returned to the mirror and placed it over the glass surface. Holding it firmly in place with her left hand, Nikki took deep breaths while moving her right fist in and out, focusing on the centre of the mirror behind the soft pillow. After a deep breath, she released everything in a silent scream, flowing all her energy out through her shoulder the way Danny had shown her. Remembering his words on attacking first, she powered her fist forward with a ferocity an enemy never expects. Her knuckles parted the soft pillow before striking the glass surface and shattering it. The pillow did its job, dulling the sound of shattering glass, the clattering of the broken shards kept to a minimum as they fell into the soft towels over the sink.

Nikki froze, ignoring the pain in her fist. She turned her head, holding her breath, listening for the lock clicking in the bedroom door. After thirty seconds, she breathed a sigh of relief and turned back to the pillow. The last shards of glass dropped gently into the towels as she slowly peeled the pillow away. Throwing the pillow in the bath, Nikki picked two long razor-sharp shards out of the towel and placed them on the toilet seat beside her. Wrapping the rest of the glass in the top towel, Nikki placed that in the bath with the pillow. She sliced and tore the other towel into strips and wound them tightly around the thick end of the shards to make a handle to her makeshift knives. When she finished, she took them into the bedroom and sat on the edge of the bed, placing the knives out of sight on the bed behind her. Then she faced the door and waited. Forty minutes later the key rattled in the lock and the door swung open. The guard leered at her as before, then stood to one side for the maid to come in carrying a silk dress.

'Please, you must wear this for Señor Delgado's return later,' she said, her eyes lowered, moving nervously around to land anywhere in the room other than on Nikki or the guard.

Nikki stood up off the bed, her hands casually held behind her. She nodded to the maid and walked towards her as if to take the dress. As soon as she was next to the maid, Nikki sprang forward, her arms spread wide. Powering them in with all her might, she stabbed the guard deeply into both sides of his chest. He looked at her in shock, his eyes wide as he stood rooted to the spot. Nikki looked him in the eye, twisting as she pushed deeper. One shard snapped off in his chest when she pulled them out. The guard stumbled forward. He opened his mouth and coughed up blood before dropping onto his knees and falling flat on his face. Nikki turned to face the maid. She put her hands up and backed away, pleading in Spanish.

Throwing the mirror shards to the ground, Nikki picked up the guard's handgun and moved into the hall. With no one in sight, she moved down the stairs, stopping at the bottom when voices and footsteps approached from the open door to the kitchen on her right. Still barefooted, Nikki tiptoed across the hall and opened the door to a dining room, twisting the handle as slowly and silently as she could to push it shut behind her.

Leaning in, she put her ear to its wooden surface. The footsteps and voices got louder and closer. Nikki stood back from the door. Controlling the shake in her hands, she placed the muzzle of the gun on the door's surface around head height. She stood there, hardly daring to breathe as she listened, her eyes locked on the door handle, willing it not to move. The seconds felt like minutes and her heart pounded in her chest. The footsteps and voices eventually died away to silence.

Nikki lowered the gun, struggling to hold back tears. Breathing heavily, she took a moment to compose herself before gently opening the door and sliding out into the hall again. The house was all quiet. She moved into the kitchen and headed for the back door, popping her head outside to take in the floodlit rear of the property. With no one about, she moved to the corner and looked down the side of the house towards the gate at the front.

It was open.

With her heart pounding with adrenaline, she made a break for it, her legs pounding as she ran along the drive towards the front of the house and the gate. She heard shouts to her left as she passed the front of the house and ran across open ground to the gate. Twisting her body to look, Nikki fired her gun toward Delgado's men by the front door. It was an impossible aim while moving and the bullets went well wide of target. The men still ducked for cover as Nikki pounded the last few metres to the open gate. She turned to face the opening, freedom within her grasp. At the last moment, one of Delgado's men appeared from the other side of the gate and jabbed her hard in the stomach. As she crumpled to the floor winded, a guard from the front of the house stepped on her wrist and twisted the gun out of her hand.

FORTY THREE

After crashing off the track twice in the dark and having to winch the truck out, Rico and his driver finally reached the main road and trundled out of the mountains into Santa Marta.

'Hey Jhon, it's Rico. I need a plane ready to take me to Bogotá now.'

Rico took the phone away from his ear while Jhon waffled on about how late it was and how hard it would be to find a pilot at such short notice.

'Jhon, hey Jhon, listen. Just shut up and listen,' Rico said, his voice going from mildly annoyed to a full on shout.

'Ok, what?' Jhon replied.

'I'll be there in twenty minutes. There'd better be a plane and a pilot sitting on the tarmac ready to go, or you will not see the sunrise. Do you understand me?'

'Yes Rico, I understand, it will be ready,' Jhon answered, his voice cracking a little at Rico's threat.

Rico hung up before Jhon had finished, his fingers

scrolling through the contacts before punching the call under Garcia's name. The phone rang an annoying amount of times as Rico waited for it to be answered. He tapped the end of his handgun on his leg impatiently while he waited.

'Rico, hold on a minute while I get somewhere quieter,' Garcia shouted over the noise in the big room.

As Garcia left the room an excited crowd counted down to the end of the election in the background. The press jostled for the best filming position for Delgado's impending acceptance speech, his lead too far ahead for the opposition to catch up.

'That's better. Rico, where have you been? I've been trying to get hold of the estate for hours,' Garcia said, looking back at the stage through the open doors to the main hall.

'It was Pearson, with Rojas's wife and some others, Colombians. They killed my brother, Felipe is dead. The comms tower is down and they took Luis Rojas and Scott Miller away with them.'

'I see. Where did they go? Have you got men after them?'

'The Rojas's and the Colombians took the speedboat and headed off around the coast. We could not follow them. Pearson and Miller took off in the Jamaican's seaplane. I think they are heading to Bogotá to get the girl. I'm about to get on a plane to come to you. Diego, are you still there?' Rico said when the line went quiet, he looked up at the airport coming into view in the distance as they descended out of the mountains to the lower lying Santa Marta.

'Yes, I'm just thinking. Fly to La Vanguardia Airport. The election is nearly over. We'll get the girl and meet you there. Refuel the plane. We'll fly back to the estate tonight. I am sure Señor Delgado will want to inspect the damage.'

'Ok, what about Pearson? He killed my brother. I want to avenge him.'

'He will come for her. When he does, Señor Delgado will kill his woman in front of him. After that, you can have your justice for Felipe.'

'Thank you, Diego,' Rico said, putting the phone away before ejecting the magazine from his gun to check the rounds in it.

FORTY FOUR

What the hell are they on about?' Danny said.

The gibberish Spanish chatter had been spilling out of the radio since they had seen the lights of Bogotá city in the distance.

'Er, let me see, something about us. Mmm, *identificate*, that's identify yourself. A load of gobbledegook, and something about Bogotá *espacio aereo*. Er, Bogotá airspace and something about shooting us down, I think.'

'Oh great, can't you fly under the radar like they do in the movies?' Danny said, looking at his phone, pleased to see the signal bar pop back up.

'Of course I can. Anything else you'd like, old man, a couple of barrel rolls or a loop-the-loop?' Scott said, easing the controls forward to lower the plane.

'No, no, just lower, mate, preferably above pavement height if you can manage that after your five lessons, sorry, four and a classroom lesson. You do know how to land this thing, don't you?' Danny said, looking across at Scott.

'Er, well, I have a fair idea of how to land a plane, with wheels that is. It can't be that much different with floats, can it?' Scott said, looking back, his face not showing his usual confident bravado.

'Water. We have to find some water to put this thing down on,' Danny said, opening maps on his phone.

He waited patiently for it to load while Scott took the plane down until it flew about a hundred feet over the rooftops.

'Right, got it. You see that three lane motorway over on your right?'

'Yes, I see it.'

'Follow that for a couple of miles. When I say, bank right, there's a golf course with a large lake in the middle, should be good, no buildings for you to hit.'

'Wonderful, and thanks for the vote of confidence. Maybe you'd like to land the plane,' Scott said sarcastically.

'No, no, Scotty boy, I wouldn't want to take away your moment to shine,' Danny said, grinning back at him.

'Mmm, I sometimes wonder why we're friends at all,' Scott replied, trying not to smile in return.

'What do you mean? You wouldn't know what to do with yourself without me. Right.'

'No, wrong, I—'

'No. Right. Turn right, Scott.'

'Oh, yes, turn right, of course.'

The plane banked right before straightening up, the golf course and its lake visible by a large dark area amongst the lit up city around it.

'Oh god, I can hardly see a thing, well here goes.'

Scott eased the plane down and throttled back, aiming for the blackest area of the unlit lake. By the time they could see the reflections dancing on its surface, the skids banged down hard onto the water. The bounce sent the plane back up into the air before it splashed down again and skipped along the top of the water.

'Well, that was easy,' Scott said excitedly.

'Scott. Island,' Danny shouted over the engine noise.

'What?'

'Island, dead ahead,' Danny repeated, bracing himself as the plane headed for the dark shadow of an island in the middle of the lake.

Scott yanked the controls, turning the plane hard to the left. He narrowly missed the island but crashed into the wooden walkway from the island to the golf course complex onshore. Wood splintered and cracked as the skids wedged themselves underneath the decking. The metal supports fixing the skids to the plane hit the side of the walkway hard, stopping the plane dead and sending Danny and Scott forward until their seatbelts snapped them back into their seats.

'Scotty, you alright, mate?' Danny said, winded.

'Yes, yes, just let me get my breath back and I'll be fine.'

'No time for that. We've got to get going. It's nearly midnight,' Danny said, kicking the door open to jump down onto the skid and hop across to the walkway.

'Hang on, old man, I'm coming,' Scott said, opening

his door and sliding down the side of the plane onto the skid before awkwardly clambering onto the walkway.

Already on shore, Danny ran across to the car park outside the club complex where a small group of cleaners had come out at the sound of the crashing plane.

'Your keys for the car, now,' he shouted while pulling a handgun from the back of his trouser waistband.

Looking scared and confused, they all raised their hands, shaking their heads and speaking Spanish at a hundred miles an hour.

Shit, I haven't got time for this.

'Scott, tell them I need the keys to their car,' Danny said, turning to see Scott catching him up.

'What? Oh right, er,' Scott said, stopping to draw a deep breath. 'Er. *La llaves*, er, brum, brum,' he shouted to them, making engine noises and motioning a steering wheel action with his hands.

'Really, mate?' Danny said, giving him a look.

'Well, it worked better than your attempt,' Scott said, running over to a terrified cleaner waving a set of keys and pointing at a crappy looking yellow Renault.

'*Mucho gracias*,' Scott said to the women with a smile.

'Give them here. I'm driving,' Danny said, taking the keys and unlocking the creaky door before jumping in.

He started the car then looked at the gearknob to find reverse, its shiny worn-off surface giving no clues. He tried right and down. The car stalled. Starting it again, he tried left and down to a grinding sound.

'Left and up,' Scott chipped in.

'No, that's first, pull up and right.'

The car moved forward when he lifted the clutch.

'Lift the little thing on the gearstick and go left and up,' Scott said, waving his hand around.

'Ok, ok.'

The lever dropped into reverse and they pulled back out of the car park. The group of cleaners lit up in the headlights, shaking their heads and looking bewildered at the two idiots that had just stolen their car. Crunching it into first, Danny bombed away from the golf course and headed as fast as the car would go towards Delgado's house in the hills.

FORTY FIVE

Garcia headed back toward the hall just as the clock clicked twelve and the voting ended. Delgado was already centre stage waving to the crowd amid flashes and yelling from the media, wanting a scoop for the morning news and papers. Moving closer to the podium microphones, Delgado prepared to start his speech. As he smiled and waved, celebrating his victory, the projected results screen behind him started blinking. Scott's planned surprise, with the help of Luis Rojas for the Spanish kicked in. The screen split in two, the real results displaying Alejandro Perez's landslide victory appearing alongside Delgado's the tampered results. Words started scrolling across the screen.

"This electoral vote has been tampered with by Scott Miller and Luis Rojas. We are being held against our will by Balthasar Delgado to hack the government voting system."

'This is an outrage. It's some sort of practical joke or political protest,' Delgado shouted, his eyes searching for Garcia to get him out of there as the press hounded him for answers.

Behind him, incriminating documents scrolled slowly across the screen. Shipments, details of government officials' payoffs, payments to offshore accounts, every detail Scott hacked from Delgado's personal computer appeared on the screen as more wording scrolled across.

"Balthasar Delgado, also known as El Diablo, is running a multi-billion dollar drug smuggling operation. There is a hidden submarine base located under his country estate on the Caribbean coast."

'This is some kind of elaborate smear campaign. Someone turn that projector off,' Delgado shouted as Garcia fought his way through the crowd toward him.

When the press blocked his path, Garcia looked for another way and noticed the police had appeared in the entrances at the back of the room. With no other option, he pulled his gun out and fired into the air three times, plunging the room into panic. The crowd started running for the exits, overwhelming the police, pushing them backwards out of sight as they fled.

'Quick, this way,' Garcia shouted to Delgado as he headed for an exit behind the stage.

They ran down a corridor towards a set of doors leading to the courtyard and Delgado's car. The doors opened before they reached them, causing them to stop and face two nervous young police officers ordered to seal off the exit. Garcia didn't hesitate. He shot both men before they had the chance to speak or unbutton their pistols from the holsters on their belts.

Jumping over the bodies, Garcia led Delgado out into

the cool night air of the courtyard. He waved urgently over to the driver of their car, who wasted no time in screeching a wide circle to turn the car around, skidding to a halt by Garcia and Delgado. As soon as they were in, the driver floored it, spinning the wheels of the powerful car towards the exit. Police cars appeared before he got there, turning sideways across the road to block it. Handbrake-turning the car on the smooth courtyard surface, the driver swerved fleeing bodies, turning into the narrow street on the far side of the courtyard, the passenger wing mirror grinding until it shattered into pieces on the wall as he drove down the narrow street at a reckless speed.

'Get me to the house, quickly.'

'Si señor,' the driver said, weaving through the back streets, his eyes flicking to the mirror to check the police weren't behind them.

'We shouldn't go to the house. The police will go there and Pearson is heading there. We should go straight to La Vanguardia Airport. Rico is there waiting for us. We can fly to Venezuela. You have friends there.'

Delgado looked across at Garcia like he was ready to explode. 'What, Pearson is here? How?'

'He attacked the estate and left with Miller and Rojas. Rico saw Pearson and Miller take the Jamaican's seaplane and head towards Bogotá. I was coming to tell you when it all erupted back there.'

'No, we go to the house first. I will get the woman and take her to Venezuela with us. Pearson has dared to attack me. I must have vengeance. I will kill her in

Venezuela, then I will have you track him down and kill him while he looks at photos of his slaughtered woman.'

'Si señor,' was all Garcia said. He didn't agree with going back to the house, but would never defy El Diablo's orders.

FORTY SIX

'Shit, we're late. It's after midnight. Delgado will know it's all gone wrong by now,' Danny said, climbing the steep sloped roads up to Delgado's house.

'Surely they'll arrest him on the spot once they see what he's been up to.'

'I hope you're right, mate, but I wouldn't underestimate a man like Delgado.'

'So what's the plan? We sneak in, knock a few fellows out and rescue Nikki?' Scott said, looking at the gate to Delgado's house as Danny drove slowly past it.

'Nope, I'm going to park just up here, and you're going to sit in the driving seat with the engine running. We'll probably be leaving in a hurry.'

'Are you sure? What are you going to do? I could help,' Scott said, eager to get involved.

'I'm going to climb over the wall and kill everyone who gets in my way until I find Nikki,' Danny answered, his face darkening with a look Scott had seen a few too many times.

'Ok, I'll stay in the car, old boy, keep the engine running ready for a quick getaway,' Scott said, quickly changing his mind.

'Good man. Here, take my phone. Try the DEA guy, Gabriel, again. Then call the police. Shit, just call everyone until you get an answer.'

Scott nodded, sliding over to the driver's seat when Danny got out and headed down the hill towards Delgado's house.

There was no time for a stealthy approach through the woods this time. Danny ran down the road at full pelt, rolling into the shadow of the trees when the silhouetted figure of an armed man appeared at the gate. He followed the wall towards the back of the property as before. Jumping to get his fingertips on the top, Danny pulled himself up smoothly until he could get a knee on the top of the wall. He stayed there in the dark, taking in the gardens and house.

There were more men to the front than there had been before. Danny counted four plus the one outside the gate, all facing the front of the house. Two more guards stood towards the rear of the house. Their backs were to him as they continued on their way to check the back garden fifteen metres away. Pulling the commando knife from his underwater encounter with Delgado's man, Danny dropped silently into the flower bed below. He glanced towards the front. No one was looking his way. With his legs tensed, he breathed deeply to fill his blood with oxygen. Turning back to look at the men near the rear of the house, Danny exploded into a run, his legs pumping as hard as they would go. He saw them turn like they were in slow motion, the first milliseconds of recognition flashing across their faces.

Danny slashed the serrated side of the commando knife across the man to the left's throat, ripping through his carotid artery and windpipe. Spinning, Danny punched the knife into the second man's chest at lightning speed. He pulled the knife out and thrust it under the man's chin up to the handle, piercing the brain. Both men were dead on the ground three seconds from turning.

Danny headed for the back door, pulling a gun from the back of his jeans. He flattened himself against the wall by the door entrance, twisting around to take a quick peep. No one was in the kitchen. Extending his thumb and forefinger off the knife, he pinched and twisted the handle, easing the door slowly open. Stepping quietly inside, Danny left the door open for a quick exit. While he checked out the kitchen, the front gate opened and Delgado's car drove through.

The window slid down to reveal Delgado in the back. 'Shut the gate, shoot anyone who approaches. Anyone, you hear me? No matter who.'

The car drove down the side of the house, stopping when the headlights fell on the two dead guards in the driveway towards the rear of the house.

'He's here, in the house,' Delgado growled, all three of them getting out of the car.

Garcia whistled to the men at the front to come over.

'You. Give me a gun,' Delgado said as they

approached.

'Listen up, Pearson is in there, he's going for the woman and we have him trapped. You two go in the front, you two in the back. The rest of you come with me. We will go in the side door. Keep your eyes open, ok. He is a very dangerous man,' said Garcia, watching them check and load their weapons before splitting up. He watched them go to either end of the house before approaching the side door.

'You. Go in first,' Delgado ordered the man next to him.

He looked back and nodded, not daring to disobey El Diablo.

FORTY SEVEN

'Ok, ok, I'm coming, ouch,' DEA Agent Gabriel Anderson muttered, stumbling out of bed and stubbing his toe on one of its feet as he headed for the ringing apartment phone.

Before he reached it, his mobile caught his attention as it vibrated an incoming call in silent mode, the number not showing up as one of his contacts. He frowned at the racked up messages and a missed call from General Dale Parnell displayed below the incoming call.

What the fuck's going on? Did world war three break out?

'Agent Gabriel Anderson,' he answered, still heading for the ringing apartment phone.

'Agent Anderson, thank goodness. This is Scott Miller. Daniel Pearson told me to ring you for help, I—'

'Whoa, hold on there. Scott Miller, the kidnapped Scott Miller? Just hold on one second, Mr Miller,' Gabriel said, grabbing the ringing apartment phone off the hook.

'Hello.'

'Gabriel, it's Pete. Where the hell have you been? It's all kicked off at the elections. Balthasar Delgado has been exposed for rigging the voting, kidnapping, and a whole load of other things. We have all the evidence we need about his drug trade. The guy's even got a bloody submarine base to smuggle drugs to the US.'

'Jesus, hang on, Pete, I've got one of the guys he kidnapped, Scott Miller, on the other line.' Gabriel put the receiver down on the worktop and turned back to Scott. 'Talk to me, Scott.'

'By the sounds of your other call, you already know that I sabotaged Balthasar Delgado's rigged election plans. Daniel and Mrs Rojas's family freed myself and Luis from Delgado's estate on the Caribbean coast. Delgado has my sister at his Bogotá house in the hills, and I've just seen him and more of his armed goons turn up there. I need the authorities there now to arrest him.'

'Where's Mr Pearson?'

'He's gone in after Nikki.'

'Ok, just sit tight. I'm going to call the National Police department. We'll be there soon, just stay on this number, ok?'

'Yes, of course, please hurry.'

Gabriel hung up and grabbed the receiver to Pete.

'Pete, call Chief Uribe, tell him to get the National Police up to Delgado's place in the hills. You've got the address in his file. Make him aware Delgado is on site, as are the two British civilians who came to see me the other day. Nikki Miller is being held captive and Daniel

Pearson has gone in to get her out.'

'They are already on their way Gab. A warrant for Delgado's arrest was issued after he fled the elections at city hall. I'll inform them about Mr Pearson and Miss Miller now.'

'Ok good. Thanks, Pete, just hurry, they have to know about Pearson and Miller. I don't want them getting hurt if any shooting breaks out. I'm on my way up there now.'

FORTY EIGHT

Danny moved faster and more recklessly than he would normally do in a hostage retrieval situation. The need to make sure Nikki was ok and his fury at her captors was clouding his judgement. He ran across the kitchen, sliding to his knees just inside the doorway to the hall and stairs. Poking the knife blade into the hall at ground level, Danny looked, searched the reflection, twisting it a tiny bit until he saw one of Delgado's men coming down the stairs, rifle in hand. Jumping to his feet, Danny flipped the blade in his hand to hold it by its razor-sharp tip. He drew his arm back, taking a second to get a mental image of the man on the other side's height and position on the stairs. Spinning through the doorway, Danny threw the knife with a whipping action, its blade spinning head over heel so fast you could barely see it. A sickening thumping noise followed a split second later as it sliced the man's Adam's apple in two and buried itself in his neck. He stumbled forward, falling down the stairs, his rifle firing as his finger jerked on the trigger.

Shit, there goes the element of surprise.

Drawing the second gun out from the back of his jeans, Danny charged forward gun in each hand, leaping over the body to take the stairs three at a time to the top. He sensed more than saw the man come out of a room behind him, and spun around to put two bullets into centre mass. The guy flew back into the room he'd just appeared from. Wasting no time, Danny moved down the corridor to the room he'd rescued Tia Rojas from a few days earlier. He fired at the lock twice before kicking the door so hard it flew open and crashed into a dressing table beside it.

'Nikki,' he cried out, moving into the room to find it empty.

A second of frustrated and confusion wiped away when he heard Nikki's voice calling his name from somewhere nearby. As he turned to exit the room, his eyes went wide as a huge Colombian guy ran towards him from the hall, his handgun raising as he approached.

Danny spun to one side as the shots whizzed past, shattering the toughened glass windows behind him into a million pieces. When he turned back to return fire, the guy was upon him. He scooped Danny up in a bear hug and continued moving forward, sending them both out the window, taking what little glass was hanging from the frame with them.

Plunging backwards towards the floor, Danny readied himself for the bone-cracking landing that was about to come. Instead they hit the pool's surface with a slap and massive splash before it swallowed them whole. When his back hit the bottom of the pool, Danny jabbed his gun into the big guy's ribs and pulled the trigger several times. He jerked and let go, holding his sides as clouds of red spread through the water. Kicking off the bottom, Danny pulled himself out of the pool. Getting to his feet, he looked slowly up at the blown-out window. His face hardened and eyes narrowed when he caught sight of Nikki being dragged away from the windows edge by Delgado. Garcia remained there for a few seconds looking down at him, a small smile flicking across his face before he walked away.

Danny's attention moved to the kitchen and the armed men pouring into it. Launching into a sprint with pool water spraying off his clothes, Danny ran around the side of the house. Levelling his guns at the living room window, he pulled the triggers seconds before diving through the exploding glass to roll up into a firing position. Two of Delgado's men turned in surprise, unable to react fast enough to avoid Danny as he emptied the magazines into them. They hit the wall before sliding down to the floor, leaving a bloody smear behind them. Dropping the empty guns, Danny ran over and picked up their M-16 automatic rifles and handguns.

'Danny!'

Nikki's urgent shriek made him turn his head. Following the sound he ran to the entrance to the dining room. Darting his head out for a quick look, Danny whipped it back as three men opened up with automatic fire. It ripped into the door frame and wall, tearing them to shreds. Seeing the holes blasted right through the wood and plasterboard, Danny stepped back into the living room. He opened fire, sweeping the rifle from left to right as he cut a line of dots across and through the living room wall. Judging by the screams from next door as the M-16 clicked empty, he'd hit his targets.

Throwing the smoking rifle on the floor, Danny swung into the dining room, or what was left of it, with splinters, bits of wall and three bullet-ridden corpses lying on the floor. When the ringing in his ears subsided, Danny could hear sirens wailing from somewhere off in the distance. He looked out the window to see Delgado's men fleeing down the drive ahead of the expected police. Powering through into the hall, he looked out through the open side door and caught sight of Nikki. Delgado pushed her into the back seat of his car before climbing in beside her. Garcia Stood by the front passenger door, he whipped his gun up as he looked in Danny's direction and let off a few poorly aimed shots. Returning fire, Danny caught Garcia in the leg and stomach, dropping him to the floor. Garcia looked back at Delgado for help as he tried to get to his feet and open the car door.

'Drive, get us out of here, go,' Delgado shouted to the driver, without a thought for his loyal right-hand man.

The car took off as Danny sprinted out of the house after it, his hand missing the door handle by inches.

'Fuck,' he yelled, anger and frustration boiling over.

Turning back, he looked at Garcia rolling around in

agony, his face angry and mood dark as he walked slowly over to him. Seeing him coming, Garcia tried desperately to get his blood-soaked hand to his gun. Just as he curled his trembling fingers around it, Danny's booted foot stepped on his wrist before he bent down and relieved Garcia of his weapon.

'Where's he going?'

'Fuck you.'

Without warning, Danny shot Garcia in the other leg.

'Argh, fuck you,' Garcia spat through gritted teeth.

'Next shot I blow your dick off. Where's he going?' Danny growled, bobbing down on his haunches to shove the muzzle of the gun into Garcia's crotch.

Garcia stared at him defiantly, breathing heavily through the pain.

'Ok, kiss goodbye to your best mate,' Danny said, his fingers pulling back on the trigger slowly.

Garcia stared at Danny's gun hand, holding out as long as he could until he realised he was really going to blow his privates off.

'La Vanguardia Airport, Rico's waiting to fly him to Venezuela.'

With the sirens getting louder and faint strobes of blue lights visible on the twisty mountain road below the house, Danny stood up.

'You're a dead man, Pearson, we will find you,' Garcia murmured from behind him.

Without turning, Danny swung the gun back behind him and put a bullet in the top of Garcia's head.

'No, you won't,' Danny growled, running out of the

gate and up the road to Scott waiting in the car.

'Get going, Scott, give it all you've got. We've got a plane to catch.'

FORTY NINE

Gabriel turned up at Delgado's house around twenty minutes after the police. He parked on the road due to the amount of police cars with blue flashing lights blocking the entrance and drive. As he weaved his way past the vehicles, two officers stopped him.

'Sorry sir, you can not come in,' one of them said.

He looked past them and saw the police chief, Armando Uribe, by a group of officers standing around a body on the drive.

'Hey, Armando,' he called.

'Gabriel, come, come. Let him through,' Armando shouted, waving him over.

'Is that Delgado?' Gabriel said, pointing to the man on the ground.

'No. He's not here. It's his right-hand man, Diego Garcia.'

'Did your guys shoot him?'

'Er, no. Hang on a sec, Gabriel,' Armando said, turning to an officer next to him. 'Jozano, just give me a minute please,' he said, turning back to Gabriel.

'He was like that when we got here. There are more dead bodies inside. Looks like a bloody war zone,' Armando continued, pointing to the house.

'Any sign of Pearson, Scott Miller, or his sister?'

'No. No white guys or women, just Colombians. We've put out a warrant for Delgado's arrest and put patrol cars on all major routes out of the city looking for his car.'

'Let me try to get a hold of Scott Miller,' Gabriel said, pressing call on his mobile while Armando sent Jozano off with some instructions.

The phone rang for a fraction of a ring before cutting to answerphone. 'Mr Miller, it's DEA Agent Anderson. Can you call me as soon as you get this?'

'Shit, perhaps they're out of service. There's no signal for about thirty miles once you get to the other side of the mountains,' Gabriel said, looking at Armando.

'Or dead. Here, give me the number. I'll get HQ to put a trace on the cell. We can get a lock on its location as soon as it pings a cell tower,' Armando said with his phone to his ear, already calling the police HQ.

Jozano headed towards the front gate, checking behind him to make sure no one was paying him any attention. He moved past all the police cars to the road outside and stood in the shadows at the corner of the property. Pulling out his mobile he made a call to the man who paid handsomely for his services. The number went straight to voicemail.

'Señor Delgado, it's Jozano. There is a warrant out for

your arrest and patrol cars are on every main road looking for your car.'

He hung up, slid the phone back in his pocket, then headed back to the house.

FIFTY

Speeding along with only the odd car or lorry to overtake in the early hours, Delgado's driver made good progress along Route 40 as it wound along next to the Rio Negro river. They emerged from the Mesa Grande tunnel and headed down towards the valley floor and the town of Guayabetal. Delgado's phone picked up the town's cellular tower and pinged with the announcement of an incoming voice message. He pressed on it and listened

"Señor Delgado, it's Leon. There is a warrant out for your arrest and patrol cars are on every main road looking for your car."

While he listened to the message, Nikki sat opposite, pushing as far into the corner away from Delgado as she could get. She'd thought about jumping out a few times, but at this speed she'd be killed or badly broken up. She decided to bide her time and wait for the right moment to kick Delgado with these bloody stilettos he picked out for her before making a run for it in the ridiculous white silk dress they'd made her wear.

'Get off the road in the next town. We need to get another car. The police are looking for this one,' Delgado said to his driver in Spanish.

'Si señor.'

The town was barely more than a small collection of houses and eateries dotted around to catch motorists from the busy road. Turning off the main road, they drove into a small town square with a few streets going back a hundred metres until the river stopped any further growth. At two in the morning all was quiet. The shops, banks and church were all dark and empty.

Nikki took her chance, drawing her leg up before stamping the tiny heel as hard as she could into Delgado's thigh. It tore through the material and dug deep into the flesh. At the same time, she pulled the door release and fell out backwards onto the road, slapping the surface with her back before bouncing and rolling over and over. With Delgado swearing out of the open car door, Nikki jumped to her feet, kicked off the high heels, and ran for the nearest street away from the square.

'Get her,' Delgado shouted, holding his leg.

The driver spun the car around and accelerated after Nikki, the hoisted-up white silk dress shining brightly in the headlights as she ran along shouting for help.

A hundred metres behind them on the main road, Danny and Scott tore through the town in the little yellow Renault. Oblivious to Nikki and Delgado being close by, they tried to ignore the engine sounding like a bag of bolts as the car trailed white smoke behind it.

'Help me, please,' Nikki yelled, running up to a house and banging on the door of a house.

The light eventually came on as she pounded frantically. Looking back, she could see Delgado's car stopping. The door opened and a middle-aged man stared at her. He kept repeating something in Spanish as she tried to make him understand they were in danger. Before they got anywhere, the man froze and put his hands up, his eyes looking over Nikki's shoulder at the driver's gun pointing in his direction.

'Do you own a car?' Delgado said politely in Spanish.

'*Si*,' the man said, pointing at a tatty blue 4x4 parked on the road.

'Inside,' Delgado said, gesturing for the man to move back before pushing Nikki after him. The driver took a quick look around at the empty quiet street before following them inside.

'Keys,' Delgado said once they were in the tiny living room. '*Gracias, amigo*,' he smiled, moving close to take the keys out of the mans hand.

There was a click in his other hand as the flick knife blade came out. Delgado dragged it across the poor man's neck before he knew what was happening. He dropped to his knees, grabbing his throat, a surprised look locked on his face as a river of blood ran down his nightshirt. Seconds later he fell on his front, twitched a while, then lay still.

With the driver's gun pushed into the back of Nikki's head, they turned to leave.

'Who was at the door?' came a woman's voice from

the bedroom before they were out the front door.

'El Diablo,' Delgado whispered, turning to walk out of the living room and into the bedroom.

'No, no, please,' came the old woman's pleading voice, followed by silence.

Delgado came back into the room and grabbed Nikki by the hair. He held the blood-soaked knife to her throat and pushed her towards the car.

Moments later they turned back onto Route 40 and continued to head for La Vanguardia Airport.

FIFTY ONE

Signal returned as they passed through the town of Guayabetal. Danny picked up his phone as it pinged with a missed call and voice message.

"Mr Miller, it's DEA Agent Anderson. Can you call me as soon as you get this?"

'Come on, Scott, give it some more welly, mate,' Danny said before hitting the redial button.

'Any more, er, welly as you put it, and this, er, how shall I put it, well-used vehicle will shake itself to pieces,' replied Scott as he eased the accelerator down a tiny bit more nonetheless.

'Scott?' came Gabriel's voice down the phone.

'No, this is Daniel Pearson,'

'Thank god, where are you? Did you all get out ok?'

'Scott's here with me. Delgado got away, and he's taken Nikki Miller with him. They're headed for La Vanguardia Airport. We're trying to catch them before he can fly out of the country to Venezuela.'

'Right, I'm at Delgado's house with the Chief of

Police. I'll try to get the local authorities to the airport and shut it down. How far away are you?'

'About twenty minutes. Just hurry,' Danny said, hanging up as there was nothing left to discuss.

They drove on in silence for a while until Scott broke the silence.

'Don't worry, old man, we'll get her back.'

'We have to. I can't lose her, Scott, I just can't.'

Before long they were heading down the approach road to the airport. Danny got Scott to pull over opposite the main building. No blue flashing lights, no police, just a few cars in the car park belonging to the night staff on air traffic control and a skeleton of security staff. The airfield itself was quiet apart from the terminal and runway lights. The only other lights visible came from a hangar a hundred metres from the main building. A small fuel tanker sat outside, refuelling a private jet.

'He's not here yet. Why isn't he here yet?' Danny said, a deep frown crossing his face.

'I don't know, maybe he's taken a different route or stopped somewhere on the way. Surely this is a good thing, isn't it?' Scott said, not knowing what Danny was going to do now they were actually there.

'Turn the lights off and drive down to the fence behind that hangar,' Danny said, his eyes never leaving the jet.

'Roger that, good buddy,' Scott said in a mock military style.

'It's just 'roger that', Scott. We're not a bunch of

truckers.'

'Oh right, yes, of course,' Scott said, driving forward in the dark.

'Here'll do, mate, pull it right up against the fence,' Danny said when the back of the hangar obscured anyone's view of them from the jet out front.

Scott did as Danny said, killing the engine as soon as they'd stopped. Danny was out of the car and pulling the furry seat cover off the passenger seat before Scott had even taken his seat belt off.

'Climb out this side, Scott, we'll climb on the roof of the car and hop over the fence,' Danny said, hopping onto the bonnet, then the roof. It popped inwards, making Scott jump as he climbed across to the passenger seat.

By the time Scott was out, Danny had thrown the furry seat cover over the rows of barbed wire at the top of the fence. He climbed over and gripped the chainlink fence on the other side before jumping to the floor.

'Come on, hurry up.'

'Nobody likes a show off,' Scott muttered, following Danny onto the car roof before swinging his legs awkwardly over the top of the fence. He lost his grip trying to climb down the other side, and fell on his arse next to Danny.

'You alright, Scotty boy?'

'Oh yes, peachy,' Scott replied, stretching as he stood up.

Danny pulled a gun from the back of his trousers and handed it to Scott.

'Safety's on, it's there, mate. Anyone gets in your way, don't think, just shoot. Remember to take the safety off first, ok?'

Scott took the gun and nodded. Danny pulled the other gun from his jeans waistband and moved along the rear of the hangar to the far corner. He looked around at the concrete where the planes parked and taxied out to the runway beyond. No one was in sight. Both the jet and tanker at the front of the hangar still couldn't be seen from their position.

'Just stay close to me,' Danny said, turning to look back at Scott.

'Roger that,' Scott said back with a grin.

Despite everything, Danny couldn't help but grin back.

'Come on, Rambo.'

They moved towards the front corner of the hangar. Danny slid his head out just far enough for one eye to see what was going on. With the hangar door open, the powerful lights within lit up the tanker and jet. Danny watched a guy in overalls unhitching the fuel hose from the jet before tucking it neatly on the tanker. The pilot appeared in the open doorway and the two men exchanged some chat. The tanker driver then waved to him, climbed into the truck and drove off towards the main building. Danny continued to watch the pilot turn his attention to the hangar. A long, thin, man-shaped shadow grew across the concrete until Rico appeared in the doorway.

'Warm the engines up, they will be here shortly,' Rico

said.

The pilot nodded and disappeared inside the jet. Rico pulled out his ringing mobile and walked back into the hangar, talking in Spanish to Delgado.

'Er, something *los motors*, the engines. Start them, I suppose.'

Just as Scott said it, the engines made a low whine and started to wind up to speed.

'Aha, there we go,' Scott said, pleased with himself.

'What about the rest?'

'Let me see, *aqui en breve*. Er, here today, no, that's not it. Soon. No, shortly, here shortly.'

'Ok, Delgado's on his way with Nikki. Good. I need you to get in that plane and stop it from going anywhere, Scott. Just point your gun at the pilot and use your charm, ok? I'm going to deal with Rico.'

'Deal with pilot, stop plane, got it,' Scott said excitedly.

'You go straight out from here and approach the door from the back of the plane. They won't see you coming until you're already inside. I'll slide across the front of the hangar and slip inside,' Danny said, looking into Scott's face to make sure he understood.

'Roger that,' Scott said, raring to go.

Already in operation mode, Danny just nodded and waved Scott off. He moved swiftly across the front of the hangar, pausing with his back against the metal panelling next to the open doorway. He watched Scott creep along the side of the plane before hopping up the steps to vanish inside. Turning his thoughts back to the hangar, Danny darted his head around the open doorway, taking a mental snapshot of the interior. Apart from several small planes, hoists and mechanics' benches, neither Rico nor anyone else was in sight. Danny moved his head across for a better look. One-sided chatter like someone talking on a phone sounded from somewhere out of sight towards the back. He took a quick look back at the plane. It looked quiet. No gunshots or shouts, which was a good sign. Turning back, he rolled around the door and slid inside the hangar.

FIFTY TWO

The inside of the hangar was very bright. Domed halogen lights hung in rows from the ceiling, lighting the way between every plane. Ducking down behind a large tool chest on wheels, Danny waited for the light to stop hurting his eyes after coming in from the dark before searching out Rico.

Where the fuck is he?

The soft metallic clang of someone dumping something down on a workbench sounded out from somewhere towards the rear of the hangar. With his gun up, Danny moved silently toward the source of the noise, his focus and the sights of his gun aligned as the two moved as one. Halfway in he froze at the briefest glimpse of someone moving between the planes before disappearing from view. Danny changed his direction, another clang from somewhere over to his left turning him again. He made a step forward and stopped.

He's playing me. He knows I'm here. He knows where I am.

The realisation made Danny re-evaluate the situation.

Where would I be? Shit!

He whipped around to the right, swinging his gun across as he moved. Rico popped up from underneath the wing of a light aircraft, his gun up, trained on Danny. From there, everything happened in slow motion. Rico shot first, the bullet hitting Danny in the shoulder a millisecond before he returned fire. The jolt knocked Danny's aim off target as he spun from the impact. His shot went high, punching a neat round hole in the wing above Rico. Aviation fuel flowed out over Rico's arm and gun as he pulled the trigger a second time. Still moving backwards from the shot to his shoulder, Danny fell back against a tool bench. Tools flew onto the floor as Rico's shot whizzed inches over his head.

The muzzle flash from Rico's gun ignited the aviation fuel. It flashed three ways in a split second, up to the wing, down to the floor, and along Rico's arm. Without taking his eyes off Danny, Rico's face contorted in pain and rage. He dropped the hot, flaming gun and charged at Danny, his sleeve still on fire. Before Danny could steady himself to shoot back, Rico launched himself at him, grabbing his wrist with his left arm to push the gun away. He twisted a full bodyweight punch into Danny's injured shoulder with his right, the fuel on his arm burning off to leave his sleeve smouldering.

Electric shocks of pain ripped through Danny's body from the injured shoulder. He was vaguely aware of Rico smashing the back of his hand on the workbench until the gun flew out of his grip, clattering to the floor somewhere behind the bench. Struggling to move his damaged arm, Danny threw his head forward with all his might. Tilting it down into the path of Rico's incoming fist. The rock hard part of Danny's forehead cracked into Rico's knuckles, dislocating the middle two, leaving his fingers sticking out at odd angles. As Rico recoiled, Danny kicked him away, pushing himself off the bench to stand up.

Both men stared at each other, awaiting the next move. Rico grabbed his two dislocated fingers, pulled them out then pushed hard, popping the knuckles back in place, his outline shimmering from the intense heat of the growing fire behind him as more fuel and the plane's interior caught light.

The deadlock broke when Rico bobbed down and picked up a large socket wrench. Danny's eyes darted to the bench. He stretched across with his good arm and grabbed a two-foot-long piece of angle iron, swinging it up in time to smack Rico's wrench away as it came in swinging towards his head. Pumped up on adrenaline and the need to avenge his brother's death, Rico came back in a flash, cracking Danny on the side of the head in a backhanded strike. Falling to one knee, Danny couldn't stop the next blow to his shoulder knocking him to the ground in agony. Next thing he knew, Rico was on top of him, wrenching the piece of angle iron from Danny's hand and pushing it across his throat.

'This is for Felipe,' Rico said, moving his face in close to Danny's.

Unable to breathe and with only one good arm,

Danny punched at Rico with no effect. With his head spinning, Danny looked towards the open hangar door. Not thinking straight, he tried to figure out where the tatty blue 4x4 had come from. It was only when Delgado stepped from the back, gun in one hand, dragging a barefooted Nikki behind him, that his mind cleared and an inner rage grew. With his hand sweeping across the concrete floor, Danny's finger touched the handle of something. Scrabbling to get his fingers on it, Danny finally gripped it and, without knowing what it was, punched it with every ounce of strength he had left into Rico's ribs. He heard a winded grunt and felt the pressure on his neck ease. Pulling his hand back, he punched whatever it was in his hand into Rico's ribs again and again.

Stumbling to his feet, Rico looked at him in shock. He coughed, the metallic taste of blood filling his mouth. The metal shaft of a screwdriver slid out from his punctured lung. A gurgling, hissing sound emanated from the stab wounds as the screwdriver bounced on the floor. Sucking in great gulps of air, Danny drew both legs up and kicked out into Rico's middle, sending him flying into the fireball behind him. Fuel covered him as he passed under the wing, consuming him in flames. He stood for a second like a human torch, then dropped to his knees before falling on his front.

Grabbing the workbench, Danny pulled himself up with his good arm. He staggered around the bench and painfully bent down to pick his gun up. Heading towards the hangar door he could see Delgado pushing Nikki into the plane. Still breathing heavily, Danny hurried for the plane. Just as he moved out into the cool night air, Delgado's driver appeared from behind the old 4x4, his gun trained on Danny. Reacting fast, Danny locked his gun in front of him and put two bullets in the driver's chest and one in his head as he shot back. When the driver hit the floor, Danny saw Delgado look at him, smile, and pull the door to the jet closed. He tried to run forward but couldn't. Looking down, he realised the driver had shot him in the stomach. Pain kicked in as his brain caught up with the shock of being shot, and his legs gave way.

No, I've got to get her back.

He crawled towards the plane as the engines wound up and it started to move away. Turning his head to one side, he saw a stream of blue flashing lights racing through the gate next to the main building, heading his way.

Seconds later he passed out.

FIFTY THREE

When his driver dropped, Delgado saw Danny standing in the doorway to the hangar, his sleeve soaked in blood as it trickled down from his shoulder and dripped off his fingers onto the floor. A second pool of blood appeared, rapidly soaking his shirt around his stomach before dripping onto his trousers. Delgado smiled and pulled the door shut. He looked through the little round window and watched Danny fall to his knees, then onto his front. Turning towards his seat, Delgado saw Nikki's shocked face as she bent down to look out at Danny lying unmoving on the floor.

'Get in that seat where I can see you, and don't move.'

Delgado pushed his gun into her stomach, driving her back down into a seat.

'Buckle it up,' he said, before limping across to his own seat, Nikki's stiletto kick to his leg still hurting.

Strobing blue lights bouncing off the buildings outside from the approaching police cars caught his eye as he sat and looked out the window.

'Hey you, pilot, get us the hell out of here, now,' he yelled, leaning into the aisle to look at the back of the pilot in the cockpit.

'Si señor,' came his reply without turning.

The engines wound up and the plane moved across the tarmac towards the runway. Delgado turned back to the window to see the police cars racing after them.

'Soon we will be in Venezuela and you will learn to obey me,' he said, growing in confidence as the plane picked up speed, leaving the police cars lagging behind.

Without warning, the plane lurched back, brakes on full and flaps up, the deceleration making Delgado fly forward out of his seat, his momentum stopping abruptly when he smacked into the bulkhead behind the cockpit. Delgado's gun slid off under the seats as Nikki jerked forward in her seat, the seat belt snapping tight to keep her in place. At the rear of the plane, the toilet door flew open and a man gagged and tied up in his underpants and vest flew into the aisle.

'What's going on? Why have we stopped?' Delgado yelled as he staggered to his feet, his eyes searching for his gun.

Undoing her seat belt, Nikki could see it on the floor between the second row of seats. She slid out of her seat and dived across, reaching down to pick up the gun. A hand grabbed hold of her hair, pulling her back violently before she got her fingers on it, the sharp blade of Delgado's knife stinging her neck as he held it against the flesh.

'Get back here,' Delgado hissed down her ear, his eyes flicking to the bright, strobing blue lights of the police cars as they surrounded the plane.

'I say, old man, would you mind awfully taking that knife away from my sister's throat? There's a good fellow,' Scott said, pressing his gun into the back of Delgado's head.

Delgado didn't move, his mind spinning as he tried to decide whether to slit her throat and go for Scott, or surrender to the police and hope he could pay someone off. He eased the knife off Nikki's neck and turned around slowly to face Scott. As he did, the police banged on the aeroplane door, demanding they open it. For a fraction of a second Scott's eyes flicked away towards the door. Delgado seized the moment, swiping his knife at Scott's neck. Scott flinched back just in time for the blade to miss his throat and slice him across the top of his arm. Acting instinctively, Scott pulled the trigger. Delgado flinched and Scott looked at the gun, confused, the realisation that he hadn't taken the safety off hitting him a second too late. Delgado grabbed it off him, ripping it out of his grip to flip it around. He flicked the safety off and pointed it at Scott's forehead. With his mind racing, Scott stood helpless as Delgado's finger moved on the trigger.

There was a loud bang as a gun went off. The front of Delgado's face simultaneously exploded all over the bulkhead beside Scott. As his body flopped to the floor, Nikki stood in his place with Delgado's gun smoking in her hand. Scott stood stunned, unable to move, until the banging on the door snapped him out of it.

'Are you alright, sis?' he finally said.

She nodded, dropping the gun, shaking, still in shock. 'Danny, is he alright? I saw him get shot.'

Scott unlocked the door and put his hands up as a dozen police officers pointed their guns and shouted at him in Spanish. They motioned them out of the plane and pushed them up against the cars while they put them in handcuffs. Looking over the airfield, they could see an ambulance by the hangar. It closed its rear doors and drove off with lights flashing and sirens wailing.

'He'll be alright, sis. The damn fellow is way too stubborn to die,' Scott said, trying his best to be cheery.

A police car raced across the airfield and stopped beside them. A man in an evening suit climbed out with a phone to his ear. He pulled it away to speak to the officers before turning to Scott and Nikki.

'You are Scott Miller and Nichola Miller, yes?'

'Indeed, we are,' Scott said, as the officers unlocked their handcuffs.

'I am Jacob Gutierrez, Villavicencio Chief of Police. Excuse my dress, I was at a charity dinner when I got the call. Here, there is somebody who wants to talk to you,' he said, handing the phone to Scott.

'Danny, er, Mr Pearson, how is he?' Nikki asked Jacob, on the verge of tears.

'He is still alive, but has lost a lot of blood. I don't know any more than that.'

'Hello,' Scott said on Jacob's phone.

'Mr Miller, thank god, are you all alright?' came

Gabriel's voice down the phone.

'Yes, myself and my sister are fine, but Daniel has been shot and is in a bad way.'

'Ok, look, go with Chief Gutierrez, I'm on my way. I'll meet you at the police station. We'll get everything sorted out and get you to the hospital.'

'Thank you, Gabriel,' Scott said, handing the phone back to Jacob.

He led them to his car and opened the back door for them. Once they were in, they left the sea of flashing police cars and drove back past the body of Delgado's driver. A large pool of Danny's blood lay on the floor just outside the burning hangar.

FIFTY FOUR

Danny finally opened his eyes after three days in intensive care, the ventilator tube down his throat making him gag. Groggy, he tried to lift his arm to remove it, only to have the pain in his shoulder jolt him wide awake. A nurse eased his arm down and removed it for him, wiping his mouth of spittle as he gagged when the tube came out.

'Just lie still, Mr Pearson, I'll go and get the doctor,' the nurse said in heavily accented English.

As he watched her leave the room, soft hands ran through his hair and touched his cheek, making him turn his head. Nikki's smiling face looked down at him.

'I thought I'd lost you,' he croaked out of his dry throat.

'I thought I'd lost you,' she replied, leaning over to kiss his cheek.

'Yes, and I thought I'd lost both of you. But it would seem I'm stuck with you for the foreseeable future,' Scott said, smiling to himself from a seat at the side of the room.

'Oh god, did he make it?' Danny croaked and chuckled, the amusement cut short by the pain in his abdomen.

'Hey, take it easy. They pulled a bullet out of there,' Nikki said, pouring him a glass of water and holding it to his mouth so he could take a sip.

'Thanks,' he said, his voice clearer. 'What happened? Delgado? The plane?' Danny said, grimacing as he tried to sit up and failed.

'Just lie still. You'll tear your stitches at this rate. If you want to know what happened, my brother was a hero. He pretended to be the pilot and saved me. Delgado is dead,' Nikki said, smiling over at Scott.

'Scott! A hero, what? You killed Delgado?'

'Well yes, er, and no. I pretended to be the pilot and surprised Delgado, but it was Nikki that saved me and killed him.'

'Shit, I leave you two alone for five minutes.'

The doctor walked in, sending the room into silence before they could answer.

'Mr Pearson, glad to have you back with us. It was touch and go for a while.'

'How long have I been out?'

'Three days, Mr Pearson. You missed all the fun. You and your friends are national heroes. The car park has been full of the world's press since the election rigging scandal and Balthasar Delgado being exposed as the drug lord El Diablo. There are pictures of his estate and submarine base all over the papers.'

'What about Danny's injuries? Will he be alright?' Nikki said, changing the subject.

'We need to keep him in for a few more days yet. You lost a lot of blood, Mr Pearson. But luckily the bullet to your mid-section only clipped your liver before exiting. It's a miracle it missed all your other vital organs. As for your shoulder, there is some nerve and muscle damage, but with rest and physio, you should be as good as new.'

'Thanks, doc,' Danny said, his eyelids feeling heavy again.

'For now it's best you rest. All of you. Why don't you go and get some sleep? Mr Pearson will be fine until you return,' the doctor said, looking at Nikki and Scott's tired faces.

They turned to look at Danny.

'Yeah go, I'll be fine,' he said, yawning back at them.

'Come on, sis. Let's get a taxi back to the hotel and get a few hours' sleep,' Scott said, smiling at his best friend.

Nikki kissed Danny and backed away to join Scott.

'Go on, bugger off and let me get some kip,' Danny said with a grin. 'Oh, when you come back, bring me food. Something greasy like a burger and chips, and a beer. Bring me beer,' he called after them as they were leaving.

'Yep, he's alright,' Scott said, shaking his head as he left.

Danny slept for eight hours solid, waking up later that afternoon. The doctor came to visit him again. Satisfied with Danny's vitals, he disconnected all the monitoring equipment and drips, and left him watching BBC World Service on TV. After a programme on the decline of the Amazon rainforest, the programme changed to Latin American news. Delgado, the election and the elaborate drug smuggling operation were still top news. They showed film of the forklift backed out of the tunnel, loaded with its stack of cocaine bricks. The camera panned around to show the rest of the submarine base and the truck slope up to the hangar.

Mmm, I guess they took the money with them when they fled, Danny thought, noticing the stack of cellophane wrapped dollars was missing.

The next report went to the Caribbean Sea. A US Navy submarine and two futuristic looking combat ships had surrounded Delgado's old ex-Russian Yasen-M nuclear submarine. The reporter went on about a joint Colombian and US operation. They'd tracked and captured the submarine as it returned to Delgado's base. The submarine reportedly went missing from the Russian Navy, presumed sunk some ten years ago.

The door opening interrupted his viewing. Gabriel Anderson walked in with another man. Danny recognised him from the TV as President Alejandro Perez.

'Mr Pearson, how are you feeling?' Gabriel said, approaching Danny with his hand extended.

'That depends whether you're here to thank me or arrest me,' Danny said guardedly, shaking his hand.

'You're ok, we're not here to arrest you,' Gabriel said with a smile. 'President Perez wanted to thank you personally for everything you have done for his country.'

Gabriel stood to one side to let the president approach.

'It is a pleasure to finally meet you, Mr Pearson. My country owes you a debt of gratitude. If it wasn't for you and Mr Miller, our country would be under the control of a tyrant. As a token of our thanks, the Colombian government would like to pay for your medical bills and for you and your friends' accommodation at the Four Seasons hotel until you are well enough to travel home,' President Perez said, shaking his hand.

'Er, you won't hear any argument out of me, thank you very much,' Danny said, not quite knowing what else to say.

Apart from asking after his health, the two men didn't stay long. They thanked him again on the way out and were gone. A few moments later Nikki and Scott entered the room, looking back down the corridor before shutting the door.

'I say, old chap, was that President Perez?'

'Yeah, is that my burger?' Danny said, the smell coming from Scott's bag making his mouth water.

'Er yes, here you go,' Scott said, fishing out a polystyrene box and handing it to him.

Danny opened the takeout box, his eyes lighting up at the double-stacked greasy cheeseburger and chips.

'Mmm, heaven,' he said, taking a big bite and closing his eyes as he savoured the taste.

'Well, what did he want?' Scott said impatiently.

'Beer,' Danny answered before taking another big

bite.

'Really, it's like talking to a child. Here you are,' Scott said, pulling a can out of the bag.

Danny cracked the can open and took a big gulp before devouring more burger.

'Oh god that's good. Old Perez, *El Presidente*, he said the Colombian government is picking up the hospital bill and hotel tab. Big thank you for services done, all that sort of stuff.'

'I say, sis, are you sure you want to marry this caveman?' Scott said.

'Yes I do. I wouldn't have him any other way,' Nikki said, leaning in to kiss him on the cheek before nicking a chip.

'Oi, get your own,' Danny said with a grin.

FIFTY FIVE

After two weeks in the hospital, the doctors deemed Danny well enough to leave and fly home. With the help of the hospital porters, Nikki and Scott took him out the back of the hospital to avoid the last of the reporters, still camped out the front hoping to get an interview. The porters insisted on pushing him in a wheelchair until he was off the premises, annoying Danny greatly as he wanted to walk out.

'Don't be such a grouch,' Nikki said, walking beside him.

Scott opened the taxi door and Danny pushed himself up out of the wheelchair with one arm, the other still hanging in a sling. His stomach hurt as he slid across the back seat, but he refused to let it show on his face to Nikki and Scott. They thanked the porter and drove to the Four Seasons hotel, taking the lift to the rooms with no complaint from Danny for a change. Once inside, Nikki and Scott started to pack for their flight later that day.

'Hey, Scotty boy, you got your stuff from Rio back,' Danny said, spotting Scott's briefcase and laptop.

'Yes, I spoke to that nice young doorman, José de Silva. Apparently he's been promoted to concierge. He had all my belongings packed up and sent by FedEx to the hotel.'

'That's great. Was it all there?'

'Everything apart from my spending money, that apparently disappeared. The Copacabana Palace hotel will not be getting a good review on Trip Advisor,' Scott said, frowning.

'That's shocking, mate, you can't trust anybody these days.'

Danny decided he wasn't in the mood to explain that he'd taken the money to help track him down after they kidnapped him.

They flew first class back to London later that day, Nikki and Danny splitting from Scott at the airport to take a taxi back to Danny's house in Walthamstow.

'Jeez, it's freezing in here. Let me put the heating on,' Danny said as soon as they'd got their things inside the door.

'Brrr, perhaps we should have gone back to my place. Sydney's around twenty-six degrees,' Nikki said, following him into the kitchen.

'Now you tell me,' Danny said, chucking something green and furry out of the fridge before checking the tea bags and coffee, struggling to get the tops off the jars one-handed.

'Here, let me help,'

'It's ok, I've got it. I'll pop down the shop on the high street and get some milk and bits,' Danny continued, the pain from his middle showing on his face despite how much he tried to hide it.

'Listen, mister, you've got to learn to let people help you. I'll go to the shop, you rest. When I get back, we can get a takeout and talk about wedding venues,' she said, grabbing her purse and giving him a cheeky grin.

'Ok, but don't get any grand ideas. The way we're going, it'll be more like a two-for-one meal at Wetherspoons than Westminster Abbey.'

'Oh you smooth-talking devil, you,' Nikki shouted from the hall as she left.

Danny moved to the living room. From force of habit, he moved to the window in the dark to close the blinds before turning the lights on. You should never intentionally light yourself up as a target. Just as the slats closed, Danny frowned and opened them back just far enough to see out through the two millimetre gap. A plain grey van had pulled up across the street, two shadowy figures in the front, short hair, sitting low in the seat, suggesting they were not tall. The interior light came on as the passenger opened the door, dark hair and classic Hispanic features highlighted in its glow. The man slid the side door open and pulled out a large Nike sports bag, its contents packing it to the max. It obviously weighed a bit by the way he lifted it.

By the time he shut the door, Danny was gone. He moved along the hall, sliding his trusty baseball bat out of the umbrella stand with his good arm. He raced for the back door, ignoring the stabbing pain in his middle. Danny shoved the bat between his legs to open the back door. Out in the dark, he slid through the hole in the fence and ran across next door's garden, heading down their alley to the front of the house. He ran across the road twenty metres from his house, approaching the back of the van from a couple of cars back. The man with the bag was nearly at his front door as Danny slid his arm out of the sling. He gritted his teeth as his shoulder screamed when he gripped the handle of the driver's side door. A couple of deep breaths and he pulled the door open and jammed the end of the baseball bat into the driver's neck, pinning him to the headrest.

'One move and I'll crack your head like a watermelon. Who are you, Delgado's men?'

The man looked shocked, scared and shook his head, putting his hands up in surrender.

The guy with the bag turned at the noise and headed back, looking up and down the road nervously from the pavement.

'No, Mr Pearson, wait. We are friends. Edgar Alvarez sent us to give you something.'

Danny looked from one to the other.

'Here, this is for you,' the man said again.

Easing the bat off the man's throat, Danny backed painfully away, eased his arm back into the sling before walking across the road past the man with the bag.

'Can you bring it in for me?' he said, breathing erratically and hobbling against the pain in his abdomen.

He opened the door and pointed to the coffee table for the man to put the bag on. Doing as instructed, the man put the bag down and pulled an envelope out of his back pocket, handing it to Danny on his way out.

'Thank you, Mr Pearson, you did a good thing for our country,' he said before closing the door behind him.

Sliding the baseball bat back in the umbrella stand, Danny entered the lounge and slumped down into the sofa, sweat trickling down his forehead. When the pain subsided enough for him to move, he tore the envelope open and pulled a letter out.

For saving my precious Tia, and all you have done for my family. We are free to live our lives once more. Thank you. Your friend Edgar.

Placing the letter beside him, Danny reached forward and pulled the zip on the bag. A long line of Andrew Jacksons printed on twenty-dollar bills looked back at him. He picked up one of the banded wedges of notes and flicked them through his fingers.

'The old bastard, he went back to the cave and got the lot before the police got there,' Danny said out loud, a smile spreading across his face.

The front door opened and Nikki walked straight past him, carrying the shopping towards the kitchen.

'Right, I've got the shopping and a menu from the Chinese on the high street. So pick what you want, get the food ordered, and prepare to talk wedding venues,' she called out laughing.

'Yeah, ok. You know, I think Westminster Abbey

might be back on the cards after all,' Danny called back to her.

'What did you say?'

FIFTY SIX

The government man known only as Simon walked briskly through Hyde Park, his breath billowing like smoke in the cold February morning air. He followed the path that ran alongside the lake and headed to a bench near the top. Simon sat down next to a middle-aged man in a suit, his face buried behind a copy of the Financial Times. He brushed a bit of fluff off his heavy winter coat with his leather gloved hand and gazed across the lake at the Princess Diana Memorial Garden.

'Good morning, Simon. What news do we have on the Istanbul incident? Has your man and the briefcase been recovered yet?' said the man without looking up from his paper.

'No, General, I'm afraid they have not. In fact, the situation may have gotten rather worse.'

'How the hell could the situation get any worse? We have an Iranian scientist killed on Turkish soil, while trying to sell us the world's most powerful compact nuclear bomb,' the General said, folding his paper up.

'It would seem Snipe may have had somewhat of a relapse,' Simon said, discreetly handing a brown envelope to the General.

'What's this?' he said, opening it and sliding out some photos of a decapitated corpse sitting in a chair, the word Jericho written in large letters in blood on the wall behind him. 'Jesus, who the hell is he?'

'Dr Heinrich Mann, he was the head geneticist for the Jericho project.'

'When and where?' the General said.

'Stuttgart, Germany, the coroners put the time of death somewhere between 6 and 8 p.m.'

'What about the others?'

'I've got men watching three of them and Pearson. It's been ten years since we disbanded the project. The others are pretty spread out. Don't worry, we'll get him.'

'I'm not the one who should be worried, Simon. I voiced my reservation about using that lunatic Snipe months ago. The committee, your predecessor and the Minister of Defence are baying for your blood. I suggest you resolve this, and resolve it quickly. Maybe you should put Pearson on it?'

'Unfortunately, Pearson is convalescing after being injured in Colombia. I have another contractor already in the field. One of the best, code name The Hawk.'

'Ah, the Serbian, excellent choice. Get it sorted, Simon, put Snipe in the ground and get that briefcase back, and do it quickly.'

'Yes General,' Simon said.

An awkward silence followed, until the two men got

up and left the bench, walking in opposite directions, seemingly unconnected to all around them.

FIFTY SEVEN

'Mmm, you're feeling a lot better,' Nikki said, lying in bed next to Danny just after they'd made love.

She ran her soft hands over his many scars to the fresh one to the side of his belly button.

'Yeah, my stomach doesn't hurt anymore, the shoulder's still pretty stiff though.'

'That's not the only thing that was pretty stiff this morning,' she said, smiling at him.

'Steady girl, it's only been six weeks, you're likely to put me back in hospital,' Danny chuckled.

Nikki leaned over and kissed him before hopping out of bed and walking into the en-suite for a shower.

'What time is your flight?' Danny called after her.

'Half three,' she called back over the noise of the shower.

'You sure about this, selling the house and moving back to the UK?'

'Yeah, I've had my time in Oz, besides, I've got dual citizenship. If you moved to Australia, you'd have to go through the whole immigration process.'

'I suppose so,' Danny said, getting out of bed.

'That is, unless you're having second thoughts,' she said, taking her head out of the stream of hot water.

The shower door opened and Danny walked in, sliding his hands around her as he kissed her neck.

'The hot water's good for my shoulder, it's feeling stiff again.'

'Oh, so it is,' Nikki said, looking down then up with a smile.

Later that day, Danny drove Nikki to Heathrow and waved her off on her flight. He drove back home at a leisurely pace, enjoying his BMW M4 and the music on the stereo. A black Mercedes caught his attention three cars back. It moved when he moved, overtook when he overtook, always three cars back, classic tailing training. Frowning, Danny took a sharp left, gunning the powerful car as soon as he was around the corner, then breaking heavily to take the next left. He powered down the road again, breaking and turning at every new opportunity, giving his tail no hope of keeping the line of sight and following him. Disturbed but satisfied he'd lost them, he doubled back to rejoin the road home.

When he reached his road, Danny drove past, circling around the block twice. Satisfied no one was there, he parked outside. Entering the house, he stood in the hall listening to the sounds of the house. Nothing. All quiet apart from the usual tick of the central heating and hum of the fridge freezer. Like a light switch being thrown, Danny ran up the stairs to the bedroom. Opening the wardrobe, he threw the shoes out and hooked his finger in a small hole at the rear. Pulling the false bottom up and out, he checked that the sports bag full of money still sat in the metal lined box sunk into the floor. Pushing it to one side, Danny pulled out a loaded Glock 17 handgun. He quickly slid the panel back and chucked the shoes on top, shut the wardrobe and went back downstairs. He sat on the sofa and looked out through the blinds at the road out front.

Holding the gun loosely in his hand, he rested it on the sofa beside him and sat there motionless, breathing calmly, his eyes locked on the road outside. An hour later, the black Mercedes pulled up outside. Two men in black suits sat unmoving in the front. Danny stayed motionless, waiting for them to make the first move.

Fifteen minutes went by and still no one moved. Danny heard a minute sound from the kitchen, an alien sound, a metallic click. The door. He was up quickly, moving to the hall, gun up, sharp focused eyes looking along the sights. He moved towards the kitchen, hearing the kettle start to boil noisily as he approached.

'One lump or two, Mr Pearson?' came Simon's familiar voice.

'I told you I'd put a bullet in your head if you ever broke into my house again,' Danny said, lowering the gun and walking into the kitchen to see Simon dropping tea bags into two of his mugs, one of his men standing just outside the back door.

'That you did, Daniel, but needs must, dear boy,' Simon said, looking at him with the teaspoon in the sugar above his cup.

'One. What's this all about, Simon?'

'We have a problem.'

'There's no we, Simon. You have a problem. I don't want to know,' Danny said, scowling at Simon as he sat down at the kitchen table.

'Nicholas Snipe,' Simon said, placing the mugs of tea on the table.

'He's dead. I killed him, so what?' Danny answered bluntly.

'I'm afraid that's not exactly true,' Simon said, pulling a thick file from the inside pocket of his jacket and placing it on the table.

Please, please, please leave a review for the Leave Nothing To Chance

As a self published indie author, I can't stress enough how important your Amazon reviews are to getting my work out there.

I love writing these books for you, it takes months of hard work to create each one. So please take a few minutes to click the book link below, scroll down to reviews and leave a short review or just star rate it.

Thank you so much
Stephen Taylor

Click to review Leave Nothing To Chance

Choose your next Danny Pearson novel

Vodka Over London Ice
The London mob clash with the Russian Mafia.
The death and violence escalate, putting Danny's family in danger.
Danny Pearson has to end the war, before more family die…

Execution of Faith
Terrorists and mercenary killers plot to change the balance of world power.
Can Danny Pearson stop them or will this be his downfall…

Who Holds The Power
As a Secret organisation kills, corrupts and influences its way to global domination. Danny Pearson must stop them and their deadly Chinese assassin in his most dangerous adventure to date...

Alive Until I Die
When government cutbacks threaten project Dragonfly. General Rufus McManus takes direct action to secure its future. Deep undercover with his life on the line, can Danny survive long enough to bring him to justice…

Sport of Kings
When Danny's old SAS buddy goes missing, Danny's unit reunite to find him. When they follow Smudges trail they find themselves on the wrong side of an international drug smuggling operation and the sport of kings, an exclusive hunt of a deadly nature...

Blood Runs Deep
Five Years Ago (Vodka Over London Ice) The London mob clashed with the Russian Mafia. Death and violence escalated, putting Danny's family in danger. Danny Pearson ended the war, or so he thought…

Command To Kill
When Australian billionaire Theodore Blazer takes advantage of todays plugged in world with sinister intentions, Danny travels to the far side of the globe to stop the world falling apart.

No Upper Limit
Journalist David Wallace is killed when he tries to find out the identity of an arms dealer known as the Wolf, Danny Pearson's SAS unit is also trying to stop the Wolf selling arms to the Taliban. When they get close the Wolf disappears forever, or so they thought…

Leave Nothing To Chance
When Danny's best friend Scott goes missing from his hotel room in Brazil, Danny pulls out all the stops to find him. The search takes him into the heart of Colombia and the clutches of a drugs baron known as El Diablo.

Won't Stay Dead
Snipe's back, awoken from his coma and with no recollection of the past few years. When the facility recondition him and put him to work, everything is fine until his memory and insanity return.

Available on Amazon

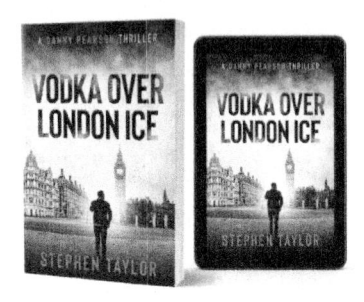

Read on for an extract from
Vodka Over London Ice

ONE

Under a cloud-covered night sky, four figures exited a Russian-built Mi-8 helicopter into the dry Afghanistan wasteland. They fanned out, taking a knee, rifles up at the ready. Their eyes scanned the terrain through night scopes. The helicopter's engines grew louder, the increased downdraft peppering their backs with stinging grit as it left. As soon as the noise died away, the team leader signalled them onwards. It had dropped them five miles from their target destination to avoid detection.

They broke into a fast tab to cover the distance. Checking his GPS, the lead signalled stop. They drank to rehydrate as streams of sweat ran down their grease-painted faces. The SAS team lay on their bellies, peeping over the ridge of a dried-up riverbed. Smudge focused through his night sight, keeping watch through the eerie green enhanced view on their target. The team's leader, Danny Pearson, ran through the intel and mission plan one last time.

'Ok, guys, intel puts the hostages in this compound here. Our objective is to get diplomat Richard Mann, his wife and his son out. If we can do that without things turning into a shitstorm, all the better,' said Danny, tapping the aerial reconnaissance photo.

'We'll follow the natural cover of the riverbed to here. On the all clear, we'll have to sprint the final forty metres of open ground up to the wall. Ok?' He paused for the teams' affirmation.

'At the wall, Smudge, Chaz, you cover the alley to the north and our exit route south. Me and Fergus will enter the compound here and extract the hostages.'

Their senses heightened as the rising adrenaline flowed through their veins.

'Remember, if the shit hits the fan, lay down heavy covering fire and get back here. I'll call in an air strike and we'll move out for extraction. Ok?'

Following the plan, they moved along the low-lying riverbed. It wound left and right until it eventually cornered close to the wall. Heads barely over the bank, they checked out the compound through their sights.

'Guard two o'clock, top of the east corner,' said Chaz.

'Roger that,' said Danny.

'Guard heading away from us up the northern alley,' said Smudge, scanning the far corner.

'I see him. Roger that.'

They watched for a few more minutes to be sure no more guards were on sentry duty. The drone images in their mission intel showed around a dozen Al Qaeda fighters in the compound.

'Guard on the wall is moving away,' said Chaz, his eyes still glued to the target.

'Ok, get set, we move on three.'

Danny paused for a few more seconds to make sure the guard didn't turn back.

'One, two, three.'

Moving as fast as they could with forty kilos of kit on their backs, the men ran tight and low to the base of the compound wall. Swivelling around they planted their backs against it, guns immediately up as the four of them covered every direction, listening.

Silence. No yelling, no alarm raised.

'Right, let's get this done by the book, guys. No heroics,' said Danny, waving off Smudge and Chaz to cover the far corner while he and Fergus headed for the compound entrance.

Two metres from the corner, Smudge lay down on his front while Chaz took a knee, his back to Smudge as he covered the rear and Danny's exit route. Moving incredibly slowly Smudge edged forward in silence in the dark. He got his eyes around the corner and looked up the northern alley. His eyes searched in the one dim light source from a lamp at the top of the alley. To his surprise a red dot appeared no more than four metres away. A guard's face glowed red as he leaned back against the wall and sucked on his cigarette.

Fighting the urge to flinch away, Smudge inched back behind the corner. He tapped Chaz on the shoulder and signalled eyes on one. Sliding off his pack and rifle he pulled his knife and turned back. Chaz stood glued to the corner, silenced gun at the ready if needed. Smudge moved painstakingly slowly into the darkness of the alley.

Bored and tired, the guard finished his cigarette, throwing the butt to the ground. He reached for his rifle propped up against the wall. He didn't get close. A hand clamped over his mouth, the feeling of cold steel against his hot neck barely having time to register. Smudge thrust the knife up into the base of his skull, killing him instantly.

'Contact. Hostile down. Mission still a go,' came over Danny's earpiece.

'Roger that. Entering compound now.'

Keeping as flat against the wall as he could, Danny crouched by the arched entrance to the compound. Reaching into his pack, he removed a little telescopic rod with a mirror attached. Extending it slowly at floor level, he twisted it around until he finally picked up the reflection of two guards just inside.

'Two. Ten yards in, right-hand side,' he whispered into his throat mic.

'Roger that,' came Fergus's whispered reply.

'I'll take those two, you cover my back and look for the one up on the wall,' whispered Danny, packing the mirror stick away and exchanging it for his suppressed rifle.

'Roger that,' came Fergus's reply, as he tucked in tighter behind Danny.

'On my mark. You all clear, Smudge?'

Lying on top of the dead guard as he covered the alley, Smudge nodded to Chaz.

'Affirmative, good to go.'

Danny swung around through the arch, eyeing the guards. He double-tapped two shots into centre mass of each guard, dropping them like a stone. Another couple of metallic pings sounded behind him, followed by a thud as the guard fell off the wall onto the dirt floor. They took a knee with guns up, covering the courtyard in anticipation of attack. No alarm. No guards. All quiet.

The two of them dragged the bodies behind a beaten-up old pickup truck parked against the compound wall. They continued towards the building that on the satellite pictures was marked as the hostage location.

'Hostiles down. Proceeding to hostage location,' whispered Danny over the mic.

'Roger that. Perimeter clear,' replied Chaz.

They moved low past the first building. Lights were on and they could hear voices chattering and laughing through the open windows. Danny moved in the lead to the door of the hostage block, with Fergus walking backwards, covering the rear.

'I'll take point, you take my left,' whispered Danny as they both stood, ready to storm the building.

'Roger that.'

Moving through the door fast, they fell into a well-practiced search manoeuvre. As they swept through the rooms, they found no guards. The reason became clear as soon as they entered the last room. Lying on the ground three feet away from his own head, was the diplomat's decapitated body. Lying next to him on their sides with their hands tied behind them lay his wife and son with their throats cut, their faces locked in the terrifying last moments of life.

They stood locked, unable to pull away from the scene for a few long seconds. The smell of death and sound of buzzing flies was etching its way into their memories forever.

'Fuck! Fucking bastards,' said Danny, the shock sending his mind spiralling. His own wife and child had been killed a couple of years ago, when a lorry driver crushed their car before driving off, never to be found. Deep suppressed feelings came flooding to the surface as he looked at the bodies in front of him, images of his wife and son appearing over the top of them as his mind overloaded with emotion.

'Fucking bastards. Bastards.'

'Mission abort. Hostages are dead. We're coming out. Prepare for evac,' said Fergus, tapping Danny on the shoulder.

'Roger that,' came Smudge's reply.

'Danny—time to go, mate.'

Dazed, Danny followed Fergus out the door without responding. As they passed the building with the lights on Danny stopped.

'Fucking bastards,' he kept muttering over and over.

'Danny! What you doin', Boss?' asked Fergus, watching horrified as Danny charged the door. Inside the shocked Al Qaeda fighters stumbled and tripped out of their chairs, trying frantically to grab their rifles. A hail of fully automatic fire ripped through the room. Blood and plaster filled the air. None of them managed to get a round off before Danny's gun clicked empty. As the dust settled, the door from the kitchen burst open and a screaming fanatic hurtled towards him with a meat cleaver in his hand. Still enraged beyond reason, Danny dropped his rifle and charged directly at the man, pulling his commando knife from its sheath as he went. A second before contact, the man flew backwards onto a bunk in a cloud of red mist, three rounds from Fergus's rifle hitting him squarely in the chest.

Danny pulled to a stop, breathing heavily with a tear rolling down his cheek. Fergus came up next to him and put his arm around his shoulder.

'Come on, mate, it's over. Let's go home.'

His face hard as granite, Danny wiped his eyes, turned and picked up his rifle. Loading a fresh magazine into it, he walked out of the building.

'Smudge, Chaz, we're coming out. Clear for evac,' he said.

'All clear, Boss, come on out.'

I can't do this anymore—I'm done.

TWO

Harry Knight sat on a kitchen stool, reading his morning paper over the white marble-topped breakfast bar. His wife, Louise, clicked around the kitchen in her high heels. He dressed immaculately as always; this morning's choice a Saville Row charcoal suit and matching waistcoat, snuggly fitted over a crisp white shirt and dark grey silk tie. His platinum submariner Rolex was just visible under shirt cuffs held together with diamond-encrusted gold HK cufflinks.

'Thanks, love,' he said as his wife put a cup on a coaster in front of him.

'Right, I'm off now, Harry. I've got to drop May off at college then I'm meeting the girls for lunch later,' said Louise, kissing him on the cheek as she grabbed her Gucci handbag and keys.

'Ok, love. I've gotta go to the club tonight so I'll be late home,' he shouted after her. He heard an 'Ok' echo back from the hall, followed by her calling for their daughter.

May's face appeared around the door to the lounge, a carefree, happy smile spread widely across it.

'Bye, Dad,' she said.

'Bye, darlin'. Have a good day,' he said softly back.

'Coming!' she shouted, disappearing out the other door.

Harry could hear Louise talking to someone at the front door.

'Harry, Bob's here. Go through, love. He's in the kitchen,' she said, slamming the front door in her hurry to leave.

Bob Angel came in through the kitchen door at an angle; the size of his shoulders wouldn't fit head-on. The ex-bare knuckle fighter was sporting a little middle-age spread these days, but that aside, he still cast a formidable shadow. He was dressed in a dark blue tailored suit. It looked out of place for a man with a flat crooked nose and hands like shovels but Harry insisted all his guys wore smart suits.

'We're businessmen, not street thugs,' he'd say.

'All right, Bob, what brings you here this early? You were at the club til four, weren't you?' said Harry, looking up from his paper. 'You wanna coffee?'

Harry got up and moved around the kitchen to make his oldest friend and right-hand man a drink.

'Yes, please, Boss. I'm round early cause we've had a bit of trouble at the club and down the Dog-n-Duck,' said Bob, the stool creaking under his weight.

Frowning, Harry put the drink down on a coaster in front of Bob. He picked up his own and remained standing.

'Go on,' he said.

'We caught one of Volkov's guys dealing in the club again last night, and Pete's had two of them approach him in the Dog. They threatened him, said he had to use them to supply the booze to the pub, or else,' said Bob, his thick cockney accent remaining calm.

'Viktor fucking Volkov, that cheeky Russian bastard,' said Harry, turning his back to Bob. He looked out the large bi-folding patio doors, thinking. A workman was jet-washing his patio while the gardener inspected his carefully manicured lawn.

'That little prick's been warned about this before and he's still takin' the piss. Get some of the lads together, track down Viktor's scummy little runners and give them a good hidin'—not enough to put 'em in hospital, but hard enough that they don't forget it. Tell them to fuck off back south of the river and stay there,' he said, turning back to Bob and spilling his coffee on the breakfast bar as he put it down.

'Shit, better mop that up. Lou will have my guts for garters.'

Bob chuckled to himself. The great Harry Knight—the man who built an empire of pubs, clubs, betting shops and property any way he could was still not the boss of his own home.

'How's the fight coming along, Bob?' asked Harry, getting back to business.

'Good, Harry, the kid looks mustard. Bets are well up. The other guy's a four-to-one long-shot. He's a good lad, happy with the bung. He'll go down in the third,' said Bob, beaming. He still loved the thrill of the fight game.

'Great. The warehouse all set up ok?' asked Harry, his mood lifting.

'Yeah, invitation only and Mark's sorted all the

security - no phones, no filming. All set up like a charity event. We've even got some talent from local clubs doing boxing bouts. Once they're all done, we'll move 'em out before the bare knuckle bout,' said Bob, taking a gulp of his drink.

'What do the figures look like?'

Bob's big hands pulled a little notebook from his inside pocket. He thumbed through the curled-up edges before finding the page he wanted.

'We've got some big boys betting. Should clear seventy, maybe eighty grand.'

'Good work. Anything else I need to know about?' asked Harry, sliding his suit jacket off the back of the kitchen chair and moving towards the hall.

'No, Boss, we're all good,' said Bob, getting off the creaking chair and following him out the door.

Harry put his jacket on, spending the time to check his appearance in the mirror. He adjusted his collar and straightened his silk tie.

'Right. I've got an appointment with the planning office. Let's see if that greasy councillor's earned his money and got us planning permission. I'm gonna see Maureen up the hospital afterwards.'

Satisfied with his appearance Harry opened the front door.

'How's she and the boys doing?' asked Bob, filling the door on his way out.

'Not good I'm afraid. The cancer's spread. They reckon it'll be weeks rather than months. Robert seems to be holding it together ok. We don't know about

Danny; he's still in the Middle East somewhere. It'll hit him hard. It's only been a couple of years since the accident,' said Harry, suddenly standing in sombre silence.

'Well, say hello to your sister and Rob from me anyway, Boss. Tell them I'll be thinking of them.'

'Thanks, Bob. Now fuck off and get some sleep. I'll see you tonight.'

Bob nodded and walked across the crunchy gravel to his black Range Rover. He opened the door. The car rocked as he got in. Harry turned towards two black-suited men standing on the drive between the three other cars. They were heavy broad-shouldered men with wide necks and flattened noses, hand-picked by Harry and Bob from amateur boxing clubs in their youth.

'Tom, bring the Bentley round. We're going uptown,' he said before turning to the other one.

'Phil, take the Merc up the Polskis and get it cleaned for me. It looks a disgrace.'

Both men got on with their boss's instruction: you didn't keep Harry Knight waiting. The white Bentley swung round and stopped in front of him. Tom hopped out and moved around to open the passenger door. Leaving the house, the white Bentley with the HK1 number plates turned left, driving through the affluent St John's Wood, heading for the heart of London and the City of Westminster council buildings.

Leave Nothing To Chance

About the Author

Stephen Taylor was born in 1968 in Walthamstow, London.

I've always had a love of action thriller books, Lee Child's Jack Reacher and Vince Flynn's Mitch Rapp and Tom Wood's Victor. I also love action movies, Die Hard, Daniel Craig's Bond and Jason Statham in The Transporter and don't get me started on Guy Richie's Lock Stock or Snatch. The harder and faster the action the better, with a bit of humour thrown in to move it along.

The Danny Pearson series can be read in any order. Fans of Lee Child's Jack Reacher or Vince Flynn's Mitch Rapp and Clive Cussler or Mark Dawson novels will find these book infinitely more fun. If your expecting a Dan Brown or Ian Rankin you'll probably hate them.

The Danny Pearson Thriller Series

Printed in Great Britain
by Amazon